"Aren't You Going To Say Something?" Kelsey Asked.

"What would you like me to say?"

"Nice day?"

"For a ride," Lucas added, stern faced. "If you hurry, you can still catch one. Otherwise, it's going to be a long walk back to the ranch. I wouldn't advise it in those boots."

"Tell me something, Caldwell," Kelsey said, propping her fists belligerently on her hips. "Do you practice being surly, or is it a gift?"

"I've got work to do." In a blatant gesture of dismissal, he turned his back to her and bent to gather his gelding's reins.

"Coward," she accused. "If you think I rode all the way up here just to watch you make another great escape, you've got another think coming, cowboy."

Reaching into a snow skiff, she packed a baseball-sized bullet and fired it as hard as she could—hard enough that it hit him smack between his shoulder blades with a satisfying *splat*.

Dear Reader,

Go no further! I want you to read all about what's in store for you this month at Silhouette Desire. First, there's the moment you've all been waiting for, the triumphant return of Joan Hohl's BIG BAD WOLFE series! MAN OF THE MONTH Cameron Wolfe "stars" in the absolutely wonderful *Wolfe Wedding*. This book, Joan's twenty-fifth Silhouette title, is a keeper. So if you plan on giving it to someone to read I suggest you get one for yourself *and* one for a friend—it's that good!

In addition, it's always exciting for me to present a unique new miniseries, and SONS AND LOVERS is just such a series. Lucas, Ridge and Reese are all brothers with a secret past... and a romantic future. The series begins with *Lucas: The Loner* by Cindy Gerard, and continues in February with *Reese: The Untamed* by Susan Connell and in March with *Ridge: The Avenger* by Leanne Banks. Don't miss them!

If you like humor, don't miss *Peachy's Proposal*, the next book in Carole Buck's charming, fun-filled WEDDING BELLES series, or *My House or Yours?* the latest from Lass Small.

If ranches are a place you'd like to visit, you must check out Barbara McMahon's *Cowboy's Bride*. And this month is completed with a dramatic, sensuous love story from Metsy Hingle. The story is called *Surrender,* and I think you'll surrender to the talents of this wonderful new writer.

Sincerely,

Lucia Macro
Senior Editor

Please address questions and book requests to:
Silhouette Reader Service
U.S.: 3010 Walden Ave., P.O. Box 1325, Buffalo, NY 14269
Canadian: P.O. Box 609, Fort Erie, Ont. L2A 5X3

CINDY GERARD
LUCAS: THE LONER

SILHOUETTE *Desire*®
Published by Silhouette Books
America's Publisher of Contemporary Romance

SILHOUETTE BOOKS

ISBN 0-373-05975-2

LUCAS: THE LONER

Printed in U.S.A.

Books by Cindy Gerard

Silhouette Desire

The Cowboy Takes a Lady #957
Lucas: The Loner #975

CINDY GERARD

If asked "What's your idea of heaven?" Cindy Gerard would say a warm sun, a cool breeze, pan pizza and a good book. If she had to settle for one of the four she'd opt for the book, with the pizza running a close second. Inspired by the pleasure she's received from the books she's read and her longtime love affair with her husband, Tom, Cindy now creates her own warm, evocative stories about compelling characters and complex relationships.

All that reading must have paid off, because since winning the Waldenbooks Award for Best Selling Series Romance for a First-Time Author, Cindy has gone on to win the prestigious Colorado Romance Writers' Award of Excellence, *Romantic Times* W.I.S.H. awards, Career Achievement and Reviewer's Choice nominations, and the Romance Writers of America's RITA nomination for Best Short Contemporary Romance.

Special thanks to Gwen Hall for cluing me in and
turning me on to aromatherapy.

This book is dedicated to my sisters in spirit,
Leanne Banks and Susan Connell.
Thanks for inviting me along, ladies, it's
been a heck of a ride!

Prologue

Like the seductive rush of hot, illicit sex, Harrison Montgomery could feel the power. The air was heavy with promise, sweet with anticipation. Alive with the certainty that the presidency was as good as his.

Refolding the dog-eared copy of today's *L.A. Times,* he angled the fine newsprint toward the bedside light. While the TV droned softly in the background, he read the column again.

With rich satisfaction, Harrison set the newspaper aside. The tedium of yet another bed in yet another hotel room along the campaign trail eased away as he breathed deep of the sound, the look, the feel of his name linked with the title: Harrison Montgomery, president of the United States of America.

It was going to happen. It was finally going to be his. The Oval Office. The power inherent with the presidency. The position he'd sacrificed everything to attain.

He flicked off the TV with the remote, then allowed himself the luxury of silence, an oasis of self-indulgent calm amid the rumble of a campaign as chaotic as a desert was dry.

Soon it would all be over.

Soon it would all begin.

Gallup, Harris, the three major networks all agreed. The endorsement he'd just read by one of the country's most powerful political columnists and CNN's recent leap onto the bandwagon proclaiming him the front-runner was the sweetest kind of icing on the cake.

He doused the light, settled back onto the pillows and welcomed the quiet and the accompanying, though false, sense of solitude. In the darkness, he stared toward the ceiling and a future he'd guaranteed with the sacrifices he'd made in the past.

The sacrifices had been many. The mistakes had been few as he'd waited for this moment. Not patiently, but dutifully. And as it turned out, wisely. A sly smile tilted his mouth. He'd let the current administration hang itself as he'd known it would. He hadn't fought the bit when the party fathers had said "no" to the last go-round. Instead, when they'd given him the nod for this one, he'd accepted the nomination with the gracious air of a man who had paid his dues. Closing his eyes, he savored the satisfaction of a job well-done.

Helen stirred in her sleep beside him. At the reminder of her presence, an unsolicited tug of regret encroached on his celebration. Helen had been one of the sacrifices he'd made along the way. Ambition for love. It had been a costly but necessary trade-off.

Again, he'd chosen well. Helen hadn't let him down. She'd been the perfect selection—the politically correct, socially savvy, appropriately connected politician's wife.

Her aspirations ran in tandem with his. Theirs was as much a business arrangement as it was a marriage. She'd contributed generously to the partnership in both talent and tolerance. And from the beginning, she'd known the score.

She'd accepted the fact that he didn't love her. She'd indulged him his discreet liaisons as a means to achieve her own end. In the process, she'd given him everything he'd ever needed. Almost everything.

Harrison Montgomery had no sons to step in where the father left off. No sons to carry on the Montgomery name.

The hollow ache of loss that gnawing fact always prompted crept in...along with the accompanying thoughts of other women. Women who had drifted in and out of his life—in and out of his bed. Three women came specifically to mind. One, in particular, intensified his feelings of regret. She was the woman he'd loved, then given up for his ambition. She was the woman who had given him the son he could never claim.

The pain came as it always did when he thought of them—the sharp sting of a loss too great to fathom, the wrenching twist of a fate too ironic to ignore. In the thick silence of this bed he shared with Helen, regret usurped his sense of satisfaction, diminished the impact of his success to date.

A sinking suggestion that success could never atone for past failures washed over him. Clench-jawed, he shook it off and steeled his mind to the future. He couldn't lose his focus now. Not when his goal was so close. Success was everything. Why else would he have given up so much to pursue the ultimate prize?

The presidency. In November it would be his. Anticipation resurfaced with a vengeance, teaming ruthlessly with adrenaline to undercut regret.

When he finally drifted off to sleep, he was cemented again in the task of achieving his lifelong goal, reveling in the prospect of his impending victory. Nothing, not the past and certainly not his regrets, could stop him now.

Absolutely nothing.

One

The last time the wind blew this hard, it had brought trouble, too. Then it was in the form of a late-spring snow catching new calves on the ground and Lucas in the foot-hills instead of the high plains where he could help save them.

The wind brought trouble to the high plains again to-day. Not in the form of snow but something just as bad: a redheaded woman with a notebook in her hand.

Lucas Caldwell sat tight in the saddle, wrists crossed loosely over the pommel, his lips compressed into a tight, hard line. Beneath him, his big bay gelding's sides heaved from the exertion of their recent climb and from the thin air at this high elevation.

Damning his rotten timing and the woman's dogged persistence, Lucas watched without expression as she wrestled with the door of a black rental compact. Clamping her hat on her head with one hand, she made her way slowly toward him while the wind played havoc with a Navaho-print blanket that looked like some flighty female's notion of a high-plains drifter's poncho.

City girl playing at country, he thought with grim amusement, catching an eyeful of her long legs covered in designer denim and knee-high wannabe cowboy boots. Little girl playing with power, he added in annoyance, as every instinct he had told him she was the reporter he'd been dodging for the past few days.

If he were a betting man, he'd stake next year's grazing rights that he was right on target. When the reporter from the *Times* had called last week, she'd come across as bold and brassy. This woman definitely fit that bill. Bold to be up here and as brassy as the red hair framing a face too porcelain to withstand the harsh bite of the screaming wind.

He'd been expecting her to show up at the ranch house, even though he'd given her an unqualified "no" when she'd called last week and requested an interview. What he hadn't expected was that she'd go to such lengths to track him down up here on the mountain.

This was not the city. It wasn't even the ranch. It was a wide spot on the top of the Big Horns, eight thousand feet up and nothing but the wind and lingering drifts of snow for company. He wouldn't be here himself if it weren't for her. Reporters were a subspecies he had little time for. That's why he'd loaded his gelding in the trailer, packed a bedroll and headed out. His excuse was checking on how the summer range had fared the winter; his intent was to avoid her.

A lot of good it had done him, he thought, accepting defeat as she closed the distance between them. She was as tenacious as a cutting horse set on singling a calf from the herd. And she was definitely trouble. Something he didn't need even a little more of today.

Eyeing her from beneath the brim of his Resistol, he gave the flashy gray felt number she was struggling to keep on top of the fiery red silk of her hair a few more seconds before it took flight. Only a discerning eye would sense his annoyance as he watched her buck the wind and walk toward him. Stoic, silent, he damned the woman's determination and the hundred yards of open ground separating him from the tree line. Five more minutes and that stand of fir would have swallowed him and any trace that he'd been here. And he wouldn't be facing her now.

The saddle leather creaked beneath him as he resettled his weight and considered making a run for it.

"Excuse me," she said, hailing him across twenty feet of mountain plains and the singing wind. It always blew on the mountain. Today, along with a gale force that twisted the poncho around her legs, doing a damn fine job of immobilizing her, it shivered with the sting of a lingering winter chill, even though it was May in the Big Horns.

"Excuse me," she yelled again, more forcefully this time, and, he noted with perverse satisfaction, with just a hint of irritation. "Lucas Caldwell?"

Only a slight shifting of his shoulders relayed his momentary urge to deny it. Resigned, he nodded. "That would be me."

"Oh, great." She sighed, sounding relieved. "The man at Burgess Junction said he thought he'd seen you up here checking things out. I guess he knew what he was talking about. I'm Kelsey Gates from the *L.A. Times,* Mr. Caldwell. I called last week about an interview, remember?"

Yeah. He remembered. And he'd have to remember to thank Cappy for sending her his way. In the meantime, he wished he felt more than weary acceptance that he'd been right about who she was—and a little less elation when a stiff gust of wind lifted the hat from her head and sent it sailing.

"My hat!" she cried, whirling, grabbing at the air in vain, and in the process getting further tangled in the poncho.

"Damn!" She spun back to him, swatting the flapping folds of wool away from her face. "It's a brand-new hat!" she wailed. She then quickly sized up Lucas, and his horse. "I don't suppose... would you... could you... is there a prayer you could track it down for me?"

One corner of his mouth twitched with the effort to fight a celebratory grin. At last, a stroke of good luck. His mother had raised him to be a gentleman. She'd also taught him to take whatever advantage he could from a bad situation.

"Never been one to turn down a request from a lady."

Touching his fingers to his hat brim, he nudged the big bay into an easy jog and rode off in the general direction the wind had taken her hat.

And kept right on riding.

She'd been had. Big-time. It took Kelsey one long, cold, disbelieving hour to decide that Caldwell had left her on the top of that godforsaken pile of rocks with no intention of coming back. *The jerk.*

As she maneuvered the rental car carefully along the paved road that wound down the side of the mountain, it took another hour to admit why she'd sent him after that stupid hat in the first place. She'd needed some time to regroup and catalog her reaction to him. The man had scared the bejesus out of her. Well, not so much the man, but the way he had affected her.

Lucas Caldwell had stunned her. His presence, his power. His innate and unconscious sexuality that was as compelling as it was quietly commanding.

As ticked off as she was with him, she still felt the tremendous aftershocks of her physical response to him. It wasn't just the way he'd sat astride that big bloodred horse with an unsettling amount of authority. It hadn't been the overall impression of integrity and strength that had escalated her heartbeat, made her mouth turn to cotton and sent a swift electric surge of arousal arching through her blood. It was the total picture he'd made: the long, lean muscle of his thighs bunched tight beneath work-worn denim and aged leather chaps; the set of his broad shoulders straining against the seams of his heavy stockman's jacket. And those eyes, shadowed and dark beneath the brim of his hat, were at once cold and judgmental, yet curiously ambivalent.

"Snap out of it, Gates," she grumbled under her breath as she negotiated a hairpin curve and prayed the brakes held until she reached the valley. "The only thing he was uncertain about was how soon he could make his getaway. He's not only an uncouth cowpoke and a yokel, he's a royal pain in the heinie."

Try as she might, though, while the heater hummed and her ears popped, she couldn't quite muster the anger appropriate to being left high and dry without so much as a "so long, it's been good to know you." And that was the worst part; she couldn't seem to shake off his effect on her.

"You could always blame it on the high altitude," she suggested hopefully. Men did not affect her that way. Not physically. Not sexually—at least not since puberty. Lord knows, many had tried. Her own sassy sexuality had proven irresistible to the masses—so the masses had told her. But Kelsey Gates was no fool, and it didn't take a mathematician to compute that her appeal had more to do with her daddy's money, than it did with her reed-slim body and toothpaste-ad smile.

Whatever the reason, the masses didn't interest her anyway. Men didn't interest her. Except for her brother, Jonas, and her crusty old mentor, Ed Wells, for the most part she found men boring, self-centered and insecure. That's why it was so upsetting that this one man—a stoic stranger who'd ridden off into the sunset like in the final scene from some B-grade shoot-'em-up Western—bothered her. He'd bothered her a lot.

It made absolutely no sense. Kelsey had one goal in life: proving herself as an individual. That meant making a name for herself as a journalist. Love, sex, male/female game playing didn't fit into the plan.

"The mystique of the West," she suggested aloud, still groping for a plausible explanation for the way her pulse leapt when she thought of Caldwell again. "The romance of the American cowboy. One with his horse, one with the wilderness. Silent, solemn, alone."

Maybe even lonely, she reflected thoughtfully as she reconstructed in her mind the granite-hard set of his jaw, the razor-sharp cut of his profile. The thin, stern lines of his mouth and the noticeable lack of smile lines etched in the deeply tanned face visible beneath the shadow of his hat, were revealing. Or so she told herself, fighting the urge to speculate at what had happened in his life to make him that way.

"So why wouldn't he be lonely?" she sputtered, attempting to work up a good lather. "He refused my interview, he left me stranded on a mountaintop—if he treats every woman the way he's treated me, he deserves to be alone."

"Probably smells like his horse, too," she muttered, irked by the twinge of compassion that had her thinking like a woman instead of a reporter. It was no change out of her pocket why he acted the way he did—except from a news point of view.

And from a news point of view, she'd come up here to expand on her story about the ranchers in the Sierras. Their plight with the leased land dilemma was similar to the Wyoming ranchers. She'd wanted to extend the story to a broader scale by including the ranchers who leased federal grazing land in the Big Horns. Lucas Caldwell, she'd been told, was the man who could fill her in.

So why would Caldwell, who was active in the Cattleman's Association, be so reluctant to talk to her when her report could only help his cause?

"Now this, *finally*," she said aloud, breathing a sigh of relief, "this is a thought process I can deal with." The reporter in her had taken over again. The woman had been relegated to the background where she belonged.

Something wasn't ringing true here. The cowboy was putting up too much resistance. He was also being too evasive. And there was something else. Something she couldn't quite nail down.

Maybe it was because he looked familiar to her even though she knew she'd never seen him before in her life. In fact, he seemed uncannily familiar. That sense of familiarity coupled with his unwillingness made for a very intriguing puzzle. Add to that her news nose that had been itching on overtime ever since he'd said no to her initial request for an interview and she knew she couldn't leave it alone. Puzzles were her life, solving them, her greatest passion. She was determined, suddenly, to solve this one.

When she reached the valley, she pulled over onto the shoulder and consulted her map. The gravel roads were the most direct route back to Sheridan. And they were tempting, but she figured she'd tempted fate enough for one day just driving up the mountain. Shifting into gear, she reluctantly pulled back onto Highway 14, conceding to the idea of the hour-long trip. Before she caught her flight back to L.A., however, she had a stop to make: the local newspaper office.

Caldwell didn't know it yet, but he'd made a mistake when he'd ridden away from her. A big mistake. If he'd wanted to get rid of her, he'd picked the wrong way to go about it. And if he had a secret he didn't want her to tap, there was no way on God's green earth she wasn't going to ferret it out now.

Lucas "Cowboy" Caldwell was about to find out that Kelsey "Ace Reporter" Gates, finished every project she started. And pity the man who believed she couldn't get the job done.

"Mooovvve over, Ollie North, a new sacrificial cow is about to be led to the political altar."

Ed Wells glanced up from the piece he was finishing for the morning addition of the *L.A. Times* and grinned across his desk at Kelsey.

He'd heard that tone of voice before. With Kelsey, it could mean anything from a hot lead to a squabble with her father. Hot lead, he decided, as he watched her, one slender hand gripping the phone receiver suspended midair, the other racing over her notebook.

Lacing his beefy hands behind his head, Ed leaned back to the creaking complaint of his aging desk chair and stretched the kinks out of his neck. "What are you mumbling about over there? You sound like you're having a cow."

Grinning like a televangelist after a Saturday-night collection, Kelsey hung up the receiver and swiveled in her chair to face him. "You ain't going to believe this one," she announced, tapping her pencil in a saucy little dance against the notebook.

A veteran of the newsroom, and a skeptic by birth, Ed recognized the flash of ambition in Kelsey's green eyes and said a silent prayer for the poor soul she'd targeted to sacrifice for the sake of a story.

"You've sung that song before, Kels. Trouble is, you're usually right. I *ain't* going to believe it."

Undaunted, Kelsey scanned her notes before turning bright eyes back to him. "You know that cowboy, the Cattleman's Association VIP I flew up to the Big Horns to interview last week to get his views on proposed legislation regarding grazing leases?"

"You mean the one who rode across heaven and earth to avoid you? Caldwell, wasn't it?"

"That'd be the one. Lucas Caldwell. Hard man to find, let alone pin down."

"If I recall, you didn't exactly pin him down."

She snorted. "Ain't that the truth. I waited up there on the top of that mountain for an hour before I realized he wasn't coming back. The man flat out did not want to talk to me. When someone is that resistant, I start asking myself questions."

"And we all know how dangerous that is," Ed mumbled.

Without missing a beat, she continued, as much to herself as to Ed. "Why, I asked myself, would Caldwell be so reluctant to talk to me when I could provide a very favorable platform for him to plead his case and that of other ranchers who would be negatively affected by the legislation?"

Ed scratched his jaw. "Maybe he doesn't trust the press."

"Maybe," she agreed, but without conviction. "And maybe he has something to hide."

"You've a suspicious nature, Kels."

"That's what makes me such a good reporter. Your words, not mine," she reminded him with a quick grin. "I've been doing some checking on Caldwell. Making a few calls. The last call hit pay dirt. That was Beth Langdon on the phone just now," she added after a thoughtful pause.

"Langdon—why does that name sound familiar?"

"Maybe because you've heard me talk to her before. And maybe—" she paused again for effect "—it's because she's a campaign worker in our illustrious leader's camp."

Ed frowned. "Beth Langdon campaigns for President Pierson?"

"Soon to be ex-president," Kelsey stated emphatically as she dug through the rubble on her desk. "Unless somebody does something to undermine Harrison Montgomery's campaign."

"Not likely. The man's pure political gold."

"Oh, come on, Edward," she groused, playing devil's advocate. "You've heard the old expression, 'If it sounds too good to be true, it probably is'?" She let that thought dangle before leaning forward in her chair. "Don't you think Montgomery is just a little *too* twenty-four karat?"

Eyes narrowed, Ed regarded her warily. "When, exactly did this train of thought derail? We were talking about Lucas Caldwell. What does he have to do with Harrison Montgomery?"

A canary-eating cat couldn't look more smug, Ed decided, as she shuffled through the papers on her desk until she dug up the item she'd been searching for.

He recognized the newspaper clipping she waved in front of him with dramatic flair. It was a column he'd written on Harrison Montgomery's presidential campaign to date.

" 'No More Pretenders—Montgomery Is The Real McCoy by *Times* columnist, Ed Wells,' " Kelsey paraphrased with a smirking nod of acknowledgment in Ed's direction, then proceeded to read the article aloud:

"Senator Harrison Montgomery appears to love his media image of a president in the making. All of America knows by now that sixty-year-old Montgomery, the son of a prominent attorney, a decorated Vietnam War veteran and a former foreign services officer to France, left his prestigious corporate law practice after the first of three successful bids to claim the U.S. senatorial seat for his home state of California. His entire life, it seems, has been preparatory to the presidency.

Well, citizens, if the crowds turning out to cheer Montgomery on his whirlwind string of campaign stops through California are any indication, the home state is proud, indeed, of this favorite son and behind him all the way. Assuming the polls can be taken at face value, his support doesn't stop at home, either. Montgomery's all-American reputation, sterling character and war-hero profile acquired in a war that celebrated few heroics, have set him in good stead nationally as well. As of last week, every major media publication—this one included—has declared him to be the front-runner in the race.

This columnist, for one, asks, *"Why not?"* America is begging for new leadership. Montgomery's claim that he will give it, has heralded him as "the keeper of the new morality." While the title may seem Pollyanna in perspective, the restoration of the concept of good old family values is an ideal the people embrace.

Montgomery personifies those values with a capital *V.* Couple his squeaky-clean image with his maturity, his charisma, his promises to lead the government away from corruption and back to the rule of the people, and you come up with an equation that can't miss.

It's a small wonder, then, that the voters are rallying to applaud his flawless past and celebrate his brilliant future. At last it appears we have a hero we can believe in—and he doesn't have to duck into a phone booth for a quick costume change to reveal his true identity."

With a theatrical sigh, she tossed the editorial onto her desk. "My, my Edward. Such a glowing endorsement. Montgomery pay you to write that?"

"Montgomery's the man in ninety-six. I don't see anything stopping him." He shrugged.

But as he watched Kelsey, Ed wasn't sure if he should be pleased by the look in her eye, or be cringing because of it. She had something on Montgomery. Something so big, she was practically popping at the seams of her tailored red silk suit with the effort to hold it in. "What's the scoop, Kelsey?"

Thoughtful, she reviewed her notes one more time, tucked them into her briefcase, then looked at Ed. "Beth had some interesting speculations about Montgomery when I spoke with her just now. Some speculations that ran in tandem with mine.''

"Cut to the chase, would you?" He made a show of checking his watch. "I'm due to retire next year. It's not like I've got time to play twenty questions."

"Kind of sad, don't you think," she continued, still skirting the issue with a speculative, cagey look on her face, "a man like Montgomery, I mean. He appears to have everything. Prosperous past, perfect present, a promising future as the next president...."

"That's sad?"

She worked her lower lip. "What's sad is that a man with that ambition and drive and boatloads of money and success doesn't have an heir to pass it all on to."

"No heir." Ed chewed on that, wondering where she was heading. "Kids aren't everything. Lord knows, there are probably days when your father wonders why he thought having you was a good idea."

Too late, he realized his teasing resulted in a blunder. He loved Kelsey like his own daughter and it hurt him to see her eyes momentarily betray her pain. The mention of Kelsey's father always struck a raw nerve. He'd never fully understood the friction there. Or why their relationship was so strained.

He cleared his throat and steered away from it. "So— Montgomery's got no kids. So what?"

"Wouldn't it be something," she said, with an I-know-something-you-don't-know evasiveness, "if there was one?"

"Was one *what?*"

"An heir, Ed." She pulled a face. "Pay attention. An *heir.* Maybe even more than one."

His *humph* told her what he thought of that notion. That Helen and Harrison Montgomery's marriage of thirty-five years had produced no children was common knowledge and old news.

"Just what kind of 'special' tea did you brew up this morning?" he asked, referring to the strange and exotic herbal concoctions she was always bugging him to drink instead of coffee.

She only smiled. It was a practiced gloat, one that made him laugh . . . until it hit him that she was dead serious.

"Think about it, Ed. What if Montgomery does have children—children he doesn't want anyone to know about?"

"Whoa. This isn't cute anymore."

"Beth and I suspect that his son—or sons—don't think it's cute, either."

"Sons?" Her look made him flinch. "You don't even know if there's *one* son, let alone two."

"Or more," she hinted speculatively, then played her trump card. "But for now, I'm only interested in one. I'll let Beth worry about the others. Take a look at this." She handed him another newspaper clipping—folded neatly and precisely so only a photo was visible.

Ed studied it, then her. "So it's an old photo of Montgomery. It's news when his picture isn't in the paper these days."

"Look again." Her eyes bright, her expression expectant, she leaned forward, elbows propped on her desk. "It's not an *old* photo of Montgomery. It's a *recent* one of Lucas Caldwell."

Ed's gaze shot to hers before he unfolded the paper and scanned the accompanying article proving her statement true.

"I found it in a back edition of a Sheridan, Wyoming newspaper along with the pictures and profiles of half a dozen other ranchers at a Wyoming Cattleman's Association meeting."

Ed ran a hand through his thinning hair as the implication took root and grew. "Holy... holy..."

"Cowboy," she finished for him, sparked by his sudden interest. "The resemblance to Montgomery is not only uncanny, it's quite remarkable, wouldn't you say?"

"I'd say," he began carefully, "that you are treading on some very precarious ground."

"Who do you suppose was a freshman at UCLA the same year that Harrison Montgomery was a junior?" she continued, heedless of his warning. "Donna Caldwell, that's who. Lucas Caldwell's mother, who just happened to drop out of school at the end of her freshman year and give birth to a baby—a boy, by the way—six months later. A boy who is now a man who avoids the press the way Donald Trump avoids Ivana, and bears a remarkable likeness to Harrison I-want-to-be-president Montgomery.

"It all adds up, Ed," she hurried on, her excitement mounting. "Montgomery would have been twenty, twenty-one at that time. He's sixty now. Caldwell is forty."

A light sheen of perspiration broke out across Ed's forehead. "Now hold on just a minute here, Kels. You're adding things up pretty fast and you're hinting at something you really know nothing about."

"What do you want to bet I find out reeeaaal soon?"

"Kelsey..." he sat up straighter in his chair. "You're talking about illegitimacy here. You're also talking about something that, if it's true, would be one of the best-kept secrets since Contra-gate. And even if it is true—"

"If it's true," she interrupted, shoving a collection of unidentifiable items into her desk drawer, shutting down her PC and grabbing her purse, "it's a truth that, if ferreted out and brought to light, could end Harrison Mont-

gomery's 'sure' bid for the presidency with one quick roll
of the presses. What would his adoring public think if they
knew he had a son he'd not only failed to mention, but
from all accounts never even claimed? All this unqualified morality he professes as fact would quickly be exposed as fiction."

Ed blew out his breath on a slow sigh. "You've bit off a
big one this time. I know you won't listen to my advice, but
I'd suggest you go easy on this. *Real* easy, you hear me?"

A light flashed in her eyes—sassy, stubborn and determined. "Easy's my middle name, Ed. You know that."

"*Trouble*. Trouble is your middle name and I don't
think I have to remind you that if you don't get your facts
right on something as explosive as this, you'll be beating
the streets for a new job quicker than you can say 'libel
suit.'"

"And I also know that if I blow the lid off this one, I'll
be writing front page instead of space available.

"Don't wait up for me, Mom," she added, the saucy
swing of her chin-length blunt-cut red hair keeping time to
her hurried steps as she made for the door. "And make
sure you miss me while I'm gone. If I'm back before the
end of the week, it'll be because I didn't get my man."

"Now where are you going?"

"I'm going back to go find me a cowboy, Ed. And this
time, I'm not letting him get away—even if I have to lasso
that ornery critter myself," she drawled in an exaggerated
cowboy twang. She spun back to face him and winked
outrageously. "Yee-haw, my friend. Oh, and keep this
under your hat, okay? I don't want anyone else knowing
about my little investigation until I have some solid facts.
And when I find them, Lucas Caldwell will be my ticket to
a byline in any publication in the country."

Or your ticket to the end of the line, Ed thought glumly as he watched her go. He didn't bother with a last-ditch effort to warn her to be careful. He'd learned early on in his association with Kelsey Gates that she only knew one way to approach a story. It was the same way she approached life: head-on, with an in-your-face brassiness, and an eat-my-dust recklessness that would either elevate her to greatness or plummet her to ruin.

He did say a silent prayer, however. Not only for Kelsey, but for this "sacrificial cowboy" she'd decided to exploit for the sake of a story, and for himself. If this thing blew up in her face and Jonas Gates, Sr.—who was not only her father, but the publisher whose signature was on both their paychecks—found out Ed hadn't tried harder to keep her in tow, not only would Kelsey be looking for employment, he could kiss his own job—not to mention his pension—goodbye.

Yeah, Kelsey had been nothing but trouble ever since she'd been assigned to him as a cub reporter a little over five years ago. Trouble, he thought, and unable to hold back a grin, one sweet breath of fresh air and righteous conviction.

Two

Elk and eagle and a dozen other wild things were prone to amble across the valley Lucas shared with them. Over the course of the past several years, whether he was drinking strong coffee at sunrise, or sipping Amaretto at sunset, he'd taken quiet pleasure in stolen moments, standing at the kitchen window watching them.

The sight that met him this morning, however, gave him no pleasure at all.

A car shot along the winding road, eating up the distance at a racing clip. Its goal had to be the Caldwell Cattle Company, the only destination in sight. And the only wild thing sharing his valley this morning was the woman behind the wheel.

The reporter from the *Times*—Kelsey something or other—was back, and this time he couldn't outrun her.

Draining the last of his coffee, Lucas glanced over at the soft gray Stetson that had hung on a peg by the kitchen door for a week now. He wasn't sure why he'd put it there—or why he'd thought so often of the woman it belonged to.

Besides being brassy and bold, she had struck him as having little more substance than her hat—at least physically. The fresh-faced slip of a female, whose slim, slight body he'd caught a glimpse of beneath the flapping folds of that ridiculous poncho, had appeared as substantial as the fine red silk of her hair.

Much more clearly than he cared to admit, he could still remember that hair, flying and tangling in the wind, the sunlight catching its fiery sheen. He could picture, just as vividly, the pink the wind had painted in her high-boned cheeks when she'd turned to him, her eyes wide and imploring.

If he'd have to venture a guess, he'd say those eyes were green, although he hadn't gotten close enough to tell. Not that he would have looked. Not that he cared. He had no interest. He already knew enough about her kind. And he knew enough to avoid them. The whimsical package camouflaged a pit-bull tenacity and a go-for-the-jugular aggressiveness that made him want to run like hell in the opposite direction. That's the reason he'd left her standing on the mountain a week ago.

It was also why it was so unsettling that he'd thought of her so often since then. Too often. That grating scrap of reality niggled at his peace of mind like a pair of new boots rubbing at a blister.

So did her persistence. His frown deepened as the car turned into the drive.

He'd known she'd be back. He'd even known it would be today. He'd just hoped he'd have had the good luck to be gone when she got here. But like winter in the Big

Horns, or calving in the spring, some things were unavoidable.

Resigned, he snagged his tan Resistol from the rack, jammed it on his head and headed out the door.

A recent rain had quieted the dust. Instead of a cloud of fine powder trailing the car up the drive, a rutted mud track settled in its wake. The car—another rental—slid to an animated stop. The driver—an equally animated redhead—shoved open the door and stepped out.

Lucas leaned a shoulder against a porch post and watched her pick her way through the puddles toward him.

To her credit, she'd ditched the poncho. To his disgust, she hadn't done the same with the boots. They were a sad waste of good leather—and as useless as teats on a bull. High thick heels, dyed cobalt blue—they weren't good for riding, not much better for walking. That only left one purpose: to show off the long, slim length of her legs, which they did with a maddening degree of effectiveness.

"Hello, Mr. Caldwell."

With a slow shift of his weight, he nodded.

"I'm glad to see we finally made a connection," she said, her smile picture pleasant. And totally manufactured.

She was good. He'd give her that. He'd yet to encounter a woman who didn't get a little chafed around the wrists when a man ran out on her. She had to be royally ticked about the way he'd ridden off the edge of the mountain last week and never come back. Yet there she stood, smiling as she joined him on the porch.

He met her eyes, perversely pleased to discover he'd been right. Her eyes were green. A vivid, sparkling green, the irises rimmed with shades of the sea and flecked with hints of amber. Framed by paintbrush-thick auburn lashes, they were bold, inquisitive . . . and beautiful.

He pulled his gaze away and nodded toward the road. "I see you found the way, Ms.—"

"Gates," she reminded him easily and extended her hand. "Kelsey Gates."

He accepted the information with another crisp nod as he grasped her hand—then quickly let it go. It was very delicate, that hand. Very fragile. Profoundly feminine. And he was far too aware of how small and pale it looked, wrapped in the dark, callused bulk of his own. Of how warm and soft it felt. Of how long—he swallowed hard, realizing it had been almost a year—since he'd touched the silk of a woman's skin, held the fluid heat of a woman's body against his own.

And therein lies the problem, he told himself gruffly. A man had needs only a woman could satisfy. He'd ignored his for too long if a fluffy little snoop like her could arouse him.

That was the worst of it. She *had* aroused him. In spades.

Even disregarding his abstinence, it still didn't compute. Except for those eyes, she wasn't even what a man would call pretty. She was as slim and sleek as a yearling filly, her skin as pale and unsuited to the Wyoming wind as the fine raw silk of her hair. Her mouth was too wide, her lips too full. Too sensual to be subtle. Too childishly innocent to be believed.

And he'd become entirely too preoccupied with the entire troublesome package.

If his silent appraisal and the sizzling contact of their joined hands had affected her the same way, however, she didn't show it. Instead, she drew in a deep, bracing breath and took a long, encompassing look around her.

When she turned back to him, her smile was wide with a pleasure more genuine than he'd like to believe. "I feel just like Hop Sing must have felt the first time he set foot on the Ponderosa," she announced brightly. "It's beautiful. I'm impressed."

Lucas shrugged, not wanting to be affected by her enthusiasm, grudging the fact that he was. "It's home."

"Yes," she said, with another nodding appraisal. "I can see that it is. And I can see why the part of the populace that doesn't live in the West is so enamored with the romance of the American cowboy." She turned back to him, her smile still firmly in place, her gaze as clear and direct as the sunlight breaking through the clouds. "I'm very pleased you've consented to show me around."

He was pleased about nothing. Not the way she sent his senses humming, not the way she'd sashayed up here, turned on her practiced charm and made him want to like her.

"There is nothing romantic about eating dust and chasing cattle," he informed her stiffly. "And if you'll recall, it was my mother, not me, who consented to this meeting."

If his gruffness put her off, she didn't show it. She just smiled again and adjusted the weight of the bulky leather bag slung over her shoulder.

"Your mother was very generous to extend an invitation. I'm anxious to meet her."

He wasn't sure what he'd expected from her. Whatever it was, she was throwing him off center by not delivering. Aggression, haughtiness, even anger wouldn't have surprised him. But this effervescent congeniality that both fascinated and captivated, drew his gaze repeatedly back to her eyes and had him stumbling to maintain a cool disdain.

With deliberate effort, he looked away. "Yes, well, I'm afraid she'd not going to be able to meet you out here this morning. Regrettably, my mother was called away."

"Oh..."

The single, almost breathless exclamation relayed disappointment. So did her expression—if he could believe what he was seeing.

"Oh, I'm sorry. Truly sorry that I missed her. And I hope it wasn't anything unfortunate that took her away."

Lucas thought of the call he'd gotten from his mother last night after a late dinner. Of the excuses she'd offered. Of his guilt over the fact that she felt she had to make them. He'd been trying to get her to go with her friends on one of those cruises for years. She'd lived alone too long in the little house a couple of miles down the road from the ranch house.

"I guess it's a package deal," Donna Caldwell had said amidst the flurry of packing and apologies. "Hazel couldn't go at the last minute. If they can't fill the slot, they lose the deposit. They need me."

And she needed to go, he'd told her at least twenty times on the drive to Sheridan to the airport. It was the timing he didn't appreciate.

He scowled, recovering his irritation that he'd been stuck with this hungry-eyed reporter whose agenda might just have a few hidden items. "The only thing unfortunate here, Ms. Gates, is that you bothered to come at all."

She cocked her head, a speculative and entirely too-good-natured look on her face. "Do I detect a little resistance, Mr. Caldwell?"

She was enjoying this, he decided as he met her eyes. And she was playing with him. With a little relaxing of his guard, he might have enjoyed playing, too. That's exactly what she wanted—which was more than enough reason why she wasn't going to get it.

He looked past her toward the mountains. "You detect reluctance. This is not a good time for me. The Triple C is a working ranch—not a social club."

"Oh, well, if that's what you're worried about, don't be. I promise you I won't interfere. And I won't get in your way. I also realize that this is your home. I don't intend to intrude on your personal life in the few days that I'll be nosing around."

He whipped his head around. "Few days?"

Again she smiled. And for an alarming, unavoidable moment, he got lost in those eyes again, and was hit by an unbalanced sensation of sinking into the equivalent of emotional quicksand.

"A week, tops," she promised brightly, reacting to his frown.

"I thought this was just an interview."

"An *in-depth* interview. Even a pictorial if I can swing it with editorial." She patted what he now realized was a camera case slung over her shoulder. "With a little luck, it'll end up as a series on the decline of the American rancher."

"Well, I hate to disappoint you, but this ranch is not in decline." He couldn't disguise the sarcasm. Not that it bothered her.

"Of course it's not," she countered easily. "Anyone could see that. But many ranches are. Why is that? That's just one of the questions I want answered. The cattle rancher as we know him is a dying breed. The need to preserve both him and the tradition is the focus of my piece."

The skeptic in him warned that she was too quick with her response. Also, her answer was too pat. The almost indiscernible flash of guilt in the wide eyes that were suddenly looking everywhere but at him added to his suspicions.

He pinned her with a look. "Why would a few stubborn cowboys be of such dedicated interest to you?"

She thought about that for a moment—whether fabricating or soul-searching, he couldn't tell. But her answer was so long in coming that he suspected it was the first time she'd given it any serious consideration.

"I guess *stubborn* is the key word here. Some people might consider it a character flaw. I consider it a badge of honor."

He snorted. "Now, why doesn't that surprise me?" Getting his mother to agree to an interview was a case in point. He was still puzzled by how she'd pulled it off. Donna Caldwell was no pushover.

A slow genuinely pleased grin lit her face as she tipped her head back and studied him. "Why, Mr. Caldwell—I do believe you might actually smile if you aren't careful."

He'd have to be careful, all right, he thought as he looked down at her. Despite his belief that Kelsey Gates was everything he'd first pegged her to be—ambitious, tenacious, and a spoiled city woman—she could catch a man off guard with her wispy feminine charm. And she'd come too damn close to coaxing that smile she was so determined to get out of him. He'd had just cause to be on guard against prying eyes and leading questions all his life. Just because he couldn't pin down her true motives, didn't mean he could discount them.

Neither could he discount his instincts. She was after something. Something that had less to do with the plight of the American rancher as she claimed, and more to do with personal ambition. He suspected he knew what she was after. In fact, he was surprised the press hadn't been around sooner. The fact that Kelsey Gates came wrapped in a bright and hard-to-resist package didn't mean he'd be a willing player in her cat-and-mouse game. The stakes were too high.

"What I have to be careful of," he said, stepping off the porch, "is seeing that the work on this ranch gets done."

He turned toward the horse barn where he knew Baxter was milling around, damned near scorched by now with curiosity and waiting for his prearranged cue.

"Bax..."

"Yo." The old man's head popped around the barn door like a bronc busting out of a chute.

It never ceased to amaze Lucas how slow the aging cowhand moved when there were chores to be done—or how fast he covered ground when it suited his purpose. A new development on the Triple C suited his purpose.

"Got a minute, Bax?"

"Sure thing, Lukey."

He detected discernible amusement in the lift of the redhead's eyebrows. She didn't say anything. She didn't have to. Her eyes, and the effort it was taking her to stall an amused grin, said it for her. *Lukey?*

Having long ago given up trying to convince Bax he'd outgrown the nickname with his first pony, Lucas clenched his jaw and watched Bax hobble toward the ranch house.

He was beginning to have second thoughts about the wisdom of turning all this curiosity over to the talkative old veteran. Bax had been with the Triple C for as long as Lucas could remember. He was as faithful as a sheepdog but he also had a mouth that ran like a river after the winter thaw.

"Bax," he said, with belated reservations, as Baxter joined them in front of the house, "this is Kelsey Gates, the reporter I told you about from the *Times*."

Grinning like a polecat with a full stomach, Bax lifted his battered hat with one hand and wiped the dust from the other one on his denims before extending it to Kelsey.

"Ma'am."

Lucas could see by the look in her eyes that she was smitten. Facing her, was a real live relic of the American West. Bax's authenticity showed in the gnarled leather leanness of his hands, in the wishbone bow of his short bony legs, the wizened face, cut deep with age and sun creases, and most of all in the tobacco-stained grin that split that face from ear to overlarge ear.

She wanted information. She was about to get it. More than she wanted, if he didn't miss his guess. Getting Bax to talk was never a problem. It was shutting him up that got tricky.

"I'm very pleased to meet you, Bax," she said, grasping his hand with such affection, the old coot actually blushed.

"Mutual, I'm sure, ma'am. Mutual," Bax said, with that candy eating grin.

Lucas grimaced, wondering again if this was such a good idea after all. Bax's rheumy old eyes held no secrets. He was as enamored with the reporter as he was with his mare Sissy's new sorrel filly.

Thumbing back his hat, he sighed and stuck with his instincts. It all came down to trust. Bottom line, he'd trust Bax with his life. Through the years, he had on more than one occasion. Bax knew the perimeters. Family matters were off-limits. If he couldn't trust Bax not to breach those limits, there was nothing or no one he could trust.

"Bax will show you around, Ms. Gates," he said decisively. Tipping his fingers to his hat, he headed at a fast walk toward the barn and away from certain trouble.

"You've got questions," he added over his shoulder, "Bax has the answers."

She caught on quick.

"But...I was hoping...I mean, not that I don't appreciate..."

When he rounded the corner of the barn, out of earshot and out of sight, she was still stammering.

And if he didn't miss his guess, Bax was still grinning.

"I'm telling you, Ed," Kelsey insisted later that night as she spoke with Ed on the phone in the living room of the ranch house, "he's elevated the word *evasiveness* to a world-class level. I get the feeling it was an accident that I made even minimal contact with him this morning before he palmed me off on a Wyoming version of Gabby Hayes. Here it is, almost sunset and I haven't seen Caldwell's cursed hide since morning."

"Maybe he just doesn't like snoopy, smart-mouthed redheads prying into his personal life."

Receiver pressed to her ear, Kelsey paced the length of the room, barely appreciating the breathtaking view of the gently rolling valley against the purple mountain peaks through the picture window.

"Guess again, oh sage one. While it was only for a few minutes, I saw him close up this time. And what I saw at close range confirms what I guessed at in a grainy newspaper photo at twenty feet. If Lucas Caldwell isn't Harrison Montgomery's son, the Pacific isn't an ocean. The hair, the build, the face—it's like looking Montgomery in the eye as he must have looked twenty years ago."

Or it would have been, she added silently, if she'd had the guts to look Caldwell in the eye. His resistance had fueled more than her curiosity. A niggling sense of guilt over her intent to expose a secret that could eventually hurt him had been working on her, too.

Lucas Caldwell may be evasive to the point of militance for a good reason but, aside from that, it was obvious he was an intensely private man. A hardworking man who probably didn't deserve the havoc she was going to wreak in his life.

"Kelsey, you're going to get yourself into ten different degrees of hot water over this."

"Will you quit stewing like an old lady?" she groused, determined to get grounded again in the business at hand. She was a reporter. Prying into people's lives was her business. She had a license to be obnoxious. Besides, this wasn't about Caldwell. It was about Montgomery. And while it was unfortunate that Caldwell would be a casualty along the way, the public had a right to know if the man who might be the next president of the United States was a fraud.

"You know I'm on to something here, Ed," she continued. Even though her reasoning made great strides to legitimize her actions, she still had to work to shove back the guilt one more time. "And when I uncover it, the story will justify the means. It's not going to be easy, though. I was counting on Donna Caldwell as my main source, and she's turned up gone. The cowboy's lips are sealed tighter than a bank vault. I suspect that the only reason I'm still here is because I've convinced him I'm working on that leased land story that brought me out here in the first place."

"So why don't you just do that story and forget about this illegitimate son business?"

"And here I thought you didn't have a sense of humor," she grumbled, covering her growing discomfort over her culpability with sarcasm.

The sound of a door opening, then closing at the back of the house snapped her head around. "Whoops, I've got to go. Someone's coming, and if it's Caldwell, I can't take the chance he'll give me the slip again. I'll check back with you tomorrow."

"Kelsey—"

"Tomorrow, Ed," she promised, ignoring the caution in his voice. "Bye."

Quickly cradling the receiver, Kelsey tracked the noise toward the kitchen.

After showering off a day's worth of cattle dust Bax had so kindly dragged her through, she'd slipped into clean jeans and a soft, gauzy, big pink shirt. Then she'd waited for Caldwell to return. During that hour or so, she'd had ample opportunity to figure out the ranch house's floor plan. It was simple in design, dominated by mission oak furniture, and was saved from being Spartan by the muted blues, grays and mauves that predominated in both the upholstery and window coverings. Artfully woven woolen rugs hung on the walls and were scattered across polished wood floors that gleamed with care.

While she knew Caldwell lived here alone, the furnishings were still overwhelmingly masculine with the exception of a single bedroom that was markedly feminine. And evidently off-limits. She'd discovered the room after Naomi, the elderly cook and housekeeper, had helped her settle into a guest room that was another representation of the masculine influence. Alone, after Naomi had gone home for the day, having informed Kelsey there was a casserole in the oven and salad in the fridge, Kelsey had taken a quick guilty peek into that room with the closed door.

White on white, lace on satin. Feminine to the max. A sensual room for all its virginal implications. And it was a total anomaly in this house that seemed to reflect its occupant's hard edges and stark, no-nonsense code of silence.

Tiptoeing on stocking feet past that room and the questions it had raised, she crossed her fingers and poked her head around the open kitchen door.

Bingo!

Caldwell stood at the sink with his back to her. Her first instinct was to rush to the back door, lock it, then race back to the hallway door where she stood and bar his escape—with her body if she had to.

On the heels of that thought, however, came the realization that she still had a problem with her pulse rate whenever he was around. The cowboy was a lot of man. More than she'd ever encountered and more than she figured she could handle on a personal level. That irritating bit of information still annoyed her. She liked to think that she could handle anything. That a man—a cowboy, to boot—could shake that conviction did not sit one bit well.

For the past week she'd worked on convincing herself he wasn't as compelling a presence as she remembered. One look at him this morning, however, standing tall and lean in his good-guy hat and workingman's clothes, and her knees had darned near given out. She had experienced a melting rush of pure sexual heat that had warmed everything from the tips of her ears to her tootsies.

Perplexed, annoyed and thoughtful, she studied him in silence. This was the first time she'd seen him without his hat. While he didn't seem quite so imposing without it, he was still every bit as attractive. His hair was thick and dark, threaded at the temples with the lightest touch of silver. A quick finger-combing appeared to be the only attention he'd given the soft matted curls. Unbidden, she thought of a dozen different kinds of attention she'd like to give it.

As she stood there watching him in the gradually fading light of dusk, though, the adrenaline that fueled the urge to corner him and the energy it was taking to bank her physical response, gave way to quiet speculation. Then to a tentative concern.

He was so still as he stood there. So silent. So weary. She could almost feel his fatigue in the droop of his broad shoulders, in the deep, slow breath that expanded his chest and pulled his blue chambray shirt snug over the broad expanse of his back. One elbow was propped on the counter as if holding the bulk of his weight; his other arm was out of sight in front of him as he bowed his head over the sink. He was either in deep thought—or, she concluded with a sharp little catch in her breath that snapped all her senses on red alert, in intense pain.

It clicked then that the water was running and that his shirtsleeve was torn at the shoulder. A closer look revealed that his jeans were patched with sandy-colored mud and a darker color that could possibly be blood.

Her heart kicked into a rock beat. "Are you all right?" she blurted out, forgetting that she was spying on him from the doorway.

He didn't turn around. He didn't even register surprise that he wasn't alone. "I guess that's a question of degree."

One of the first things she had noticed about Lucas Caldwell was that for such a big man, his voice was surprisingly soft. Not tentative, not indecisive, but smooth and mellow. Whiskey smooth. Sunset mellow.

"Degree?" she repeated, frowning at the realization that the voice she'd been anticipating was textured with a gravelly roughness—as if breathing and speaking simultaneously were a major effort.

"It could have been worse."

"Which implies to me that it's bad enough," she concluded, bolting across the kitchen and joining him at the sink.

She'd never been good with blood. And when she saw Caldwell's blood—lots of it—pooling with the water and swirling down the drain in a startling ribbon of crimson, her knees threatened to give out on her for the second time that day.

Three

———

"Oh, sweet Lord," she whispered, when she could form the words. "What happened? Never mind. What can I do?"

"Just stay out of my way."

It wasn't a growl exactly. It was more like an oath and it held less warning than it did grim determination.

Past the worst of her shock, instinct took over. "Look, cowboy. This is no time to play one against the world. You need help. I can provide it."

His skin was ghostly pale beneath the smear of mud and sweat when he looked over his shoulder at her. He swept her face, then her body with a quick, measuring assessment. "Wouldn't want to bleed all over your fancy shirt."

"Screw the shirt, Caldwell. Just stop with the attitude and let me help you."

When he stubbornly remained silent, she sized up the situation for herself. The gash on the back of his hand was ugly and swollen. Not to mention bleeding profusely. The sticky blood matted on his sleeve and plastering it to his forearm indicated more damage to be uncovered.

She swallowed back a wave of queasiness, refusing to give in to it. "We've got to get this off of you," she said decisively.

Without waiting for permission, she slipped in front of him and began unceremoniously tugging his shirttails out of his jeans.

"What the—"

"Shut up," she snapped, batting his uninjured hand away and making fast work of the buttons on his shirt. "If you're not smart enough to know you've got a problem, then you just lost your say in how we take care of it."

Her take-charge tactics had worked on more than one occasion, but never as effectively as they did now. Six feet and two-hundred-plus pounds of speechless cowboy stared down at her in acquiescent silence as she stripped the shirt from his shoulders and off one arm.

His reluctant compliance, which implied an equally reluctant measure of trust on his part, brought out an unsettling tenderness in her. This was clearly a man who was not used to having anyone share the load. Yet he was allowing her to help him. She didn't want to think about why that affected her. She didn't want to think about what it meant. And she didn't want to analyze why she felt this almost-panicky concern for his well-being.

She just wanted a story, she reminded herself. Still, she found herself being cautious and careful as she gently peeled the other sleeve away from his injured arm. She bit back another gasp when she got a look at the angry-looking half-moon-shaped wound on his forearm.

"Again, with the blood," she muttered then drew a deep breath, determined not to let it get to her. "What the devil happened?'' she managed in a choked whisper after making herself examine the extent of the damage.

He didn't flinch, but she felt the tensing of his muscle beneath her hands as she guided his arm under the cold running water.

"Nothing that doesn't happen half a dozen times a year. I got on the wrong side of a horse and a hoof."

The wounds were ugly and raw and indicated to her that there was a lot more to the story than his dismissive response suggested. So did his pallor and the grim set of his mouth that relayed his pain.

"Has anyone ever told you that you have a gift for understatement, Caldwell?"

He only grunted.

"Yeah. My sentiments exactly."

Feeling a little steadier now that she could see that the damage, though bad, wasn't as extensive as the flow of blood indicated, she shut off the faucet.

"Can you move it?"

With effort he flexed his hand.

Her best guess was that nothing was broken. She wasn't going to be satisfied, though, until he saw a doctor. Snagging a handful of paper towels, she patted his arm and hand dry, then held pressure over both wounds that were still seeping blood.

"Do you have a first-aid kit around here? Well, do you?" she insisted, losing both her patience with herself for becoming so concerned about him and her compassion for him when he stood silent and staring above her. "It's not that tough a question."

With a glare and a grumble, he gave the information. "Top shelf, second door on the left."

Without ceremony, she tugged a chair over to the cabinets, climbed up on it then rummaged through the contents of the top shelf until she came up with the first-aid kit.

"Sit," she ordered, pointing to the kitchen table as her feet hit the kitchen floor. "And hold pressure on that arm."

His glare intensified. She waited him out until finally, with a muttered oath and a roll of his eyes, he stalked to the table and sat.

"Don't mess with me, Caldwell," she advised, reclaiming a cool emotional distance as she dragged the chair directly in front of his and plopped down. "Because you're not going to win this one. It's this nurturing instinct that kicks in when I see anything wounded. Dogs, cats... cowboys," she added with a straight face and a quick glance.

And it was just instinct and nothing more, she reaffirmed silently. It certainly wasn't that she cared anything about him. For heaven's sake, she hardly knew him. And what she did know about him warned her that any investment of emotion would be a waste of energy and time. He was about as receptive to her help as a lone wolf to an outsider helping himself to claimed territory.

He didn't fight her, though, when she leaned over his arm and peeled back the paper toweling. He couldn't, however, resist a well-placed jab.

"Nurturing is not a quality that comes to mind when I look at you."

His statement surprised her. Not only the fact that he'd made it, but that he'd admit that he'd been looking at her—or for that matter, bothering to form any opinions.

With great effort, she kept her head down and her eyes on what she was doing. She didn't have to see his face to know he was scowling. She didn't have to look in a mirror to know her face was set in the same grim lines. "Yeah, well, there's a lot more to me than meets the eye."

A long pause followed. Then a soft and reluctant "So I've suspected."

She raised her head and met his gaze over his extended arm—a direct contact she'd been avoiding. With good reason.

They were quite something, those eyes. Like those of a tense, lone wolf he was beginning to remind her of, they were a clear, vivid topaz shot through with liberal shades of cinnamon, bronze and gold. Beautiful, noble. Proud. And like the eyes of a predator, watchful and alert.

As she sat there, immobilized by the power, spellbound by the intensity, she understood why she'd been avoiding them for so long. Anger, impatience, even disgust she could have dealt with. While she suspected all those emotions were there, they were veiled by an awareness that sent her senses humming and her pulse tripping at an erratic, dizzying pace.

His eyes relayed not only an awareness of her as a woman, but his somber, probing gaze seemed to penetrate a barrier she'd worked years to erect and was able to see straight into the secrets of her soul...to the insecurity and self-doubt. To the truth that she was running scared from failure and covering it all with false bravado.

The sensation of exposure and the weakness she felt because of it, disarmed her. She looked away, compensating as she always did when she felt defensive, with sarcasm. "I suppose it would be a stretch to take that as a compliment."

When he neither confirmed nor denied her flip remark, she grabbed the peroxide. Fighting to keep her hand from trembling, she trickled the antiseptic over the open wound.

He caught his breath on a hiss.

She didn't want to feel admiration. Or compassion. Not for this man. She couldn't afford it. Not when with one look he had managed to make her feel as if she were the one with the secret in need of protecting.

Combatting an insecurity she refused to give in to, and a compassion she wouldn't allow, she reacted with just enough bite to set her back on course. "I'm impressed, cowboy. And you didn't even need a bullet to bite on."

Her remark evidently set him back on the straight and narrow, too. All the softness had left his eyes.

"Oh, my..." she said, gauging the depth of his scowl. "If looks could kill."

Beads of sweat had broken out on his forehead. "Just warn me next time, okay?"

His voice was gruff with pain and hard-fought control. Guilt almost got the best of her. Not that she'd admit it. And not that she'd give in. She tipped the bottle again.

Another harsh breath escaped him. "Florence Nightingale you're not," he managed between clenched teeth.

"Nope," she agreed cheerfully. "I'm not. But I am effective." With effort, she concentrated on her handiwork, studying his injuries with a critical eye. "I think we can call them clean. The next step is to get you stitched up. How far is it to the closest emergency room?"

"I don't need an emergency room. And it doesn't need stitches. Just slap a Band-Aid on it and call it a day."

His tone held a finality she didn't dare question.

"Fine," she said, up to here with his code-of-the-West machismo and unsettled by his confusing signals of hostility and... And what? she asked herself in frustration. In the next breath, she reminded herself she didn't care what it was. She was here for a story, not a character study. And she certainly didn't intend to cultivate a relationship. Just as she didn't plan on scratching the physical itch he'd started with his lean cowboy looks and overpowering sexuality.

And that's what this all boiled down to, she told herself rationally. She was mixing apples and oranges and getting chemistry confused with caring.

"Play it your way, Caldwell. Just don't blame me if you get a couple of ugly scars out of the deal."

The sound he made could have passed for a laugh if he'd been smiling. Which of course he wasn't.

She dumped a half a dozen Band-Aids onto the table.

"On second thought . . ." He rose so quickly, they narrowly missed cracking heads. More quickly than the situation warranted, yet somehow not fast enough to suit him. "That can wait until after I shower."

"Suit yourself," she said with a shrug. She could be just as perverse as he could and decided to prove it in the next breath. "If you want to play fast and loose with your own well-being, by all means, knock yourself out. It's no skin off my knuckles."

And that's a fact, she assured herself. She had no interest in the surly son of a gun other than to get her story. Which was why she was as surprised as he looked when she blurted out, "But just tell me something, would you? Why is it that you walk away from every situation you feel is confrontational?"

She was still wondering where that accusation had come from when they faced off in the fading light of dusk. The look in his eyes told her he was wondering the same thing.

She'd already established that there was no emotional investment here. What they were dealing with was an injured hand. And just maybe, they were also dealing with the leftover baggage of him leaving her stranded on the mountain a week ago and dumping her on Bax this morning.

What they were *not* dealing with, she insisted, as she met him glare for glare, was some complex emotional or sexual entanglement.

At least he wasn't. Or was he?

The shock and the accompanying absurdity of the notion stopped her cold. And in that instant, she got the distinct impression that the same thought had occurred to him, too.

He stared at her in edgy silence. When he finally spoke, only sheer will kept her from flinching. "I do not walk away from every confrontational situation, Ms. Gates. Just the ones that aren't worth the effort."

It was a deliberate shot meant to maintain a definable distance between them. Surprisingly, it stung. But then, she had no doubt it was supposed to. He was trying to make it clear that not only were her questions intolerable, so was her presence. So was the idea that there could possibly be any "situation"—confrontational or otherwise—between them.

Except that it was beginning to sink in that the word *situation* was a benign summation of what was really occurring.

She searched his eyes, alternately denying it and wondering when things had actually evolved to a mutual man/woman awareness. She'd thought it was only one-sided.

Maybe it had been when she'd stripped off his shirt and felt the slight quiver of his heated skin beneath her hands, the dark silken curls on his chest brush the back of her trembling fingers. Maybe it had been when the unsteady warmth of his breath had fanned the top of her head as he'd stood over her, exhausted, acquiescent and in pain. Maybe it was the oddly erotic implied intimacy as his blood had spilled across her hands and splattered on her blouse.

And just maybe it had been there all along and she'd refused to see it.

She hadn't wanted to believe the flinty fire in his eyes was hunger. She hadn't a reason to assume it was desire.

She couldn't *let* herself conclude that it was need.

But as she sat there, watching him walk stiffly out of the kitchen, the lean muscles of his bare back tense and rippling, the dark hair at his nape curling against the sun-bronzed tint of his skin, it was a possibility she was having more and more trouble denying.

Lucas Caldwell was attracted to her? Maybe even as attracted to her as she was to him?

"Oh, damn," she whispered into the empty room as the notion set in. "Oh, hot who'd-a-thunk-it damn."

Thoughtful, stunned, maybe even a little afraid of what it all meant, she couldn't imagine a conclusion that would have surprised her more. *Lucas Caldwell, attracted to her.* The idea that the river might flow both ways took firmer root and sank deeper.

Slumping back in the chair, Kelsey stared blankly at her stocking feet, then at the specks of Lucas Caldwell's blood that had stained her shirt. Deep in thought, she let her gaze wander without direction—until it snagged on the hat rack by the door.

It was then that she noticed the gray Stetson she'd given up for lost was hanging on a peg next to his Resistol.

"Kelsey Marie Gates," she murmured in disbelief as she stared at those two hats hanging side by side. "What have you chewed off for yourself this time?"

Lucas stood under the hot shower longer than was necessary. Longer even, than was wise. But he needed time. Time to wash the fresh, yet enticingly exotic scent of her from his skin. Time to drown out the other arresting fragrance that lingered in the bathroom from the shower she'd taken earlier. Time to regroup and deal with what was happening.

What the hell *is* happening, Caldwell? he asked himself. He tipped his face to the spray and grudgingly admitted that he had a problem. A problem that had less to do with annoyance than it did with awareness. Awareness edged with the sweet, destructive tug of desire.

He hadn't been prepared for the things the woman did to his mind. Or his body. The way she smelled, like spring and sunshine and an illusive, yet distinctly exotic fragrance which at the same time stimulated and soothed him. The way she looked, intense and concerned, stern and judgmental, sexy and shy, set him on ten different edges. All of them razor sharp. The way she'd touched him, with delicate hands and gentle care, stirred a softness in him he'd never intended to feel for another woman.

He'd learned the pitfalls of that particular error the hard way. He didn't intend to get sucked in again. Yet the damn woman managed to frustrate him to the brink of anger, and at the same time arouse him to the point of distraction. His run-in with Glow Par this afternoon was proof of that. Catching the stallion's hoof was a fool's trick if ever there was one.

He flexed his battered hand, then muttered an oath when he saw both it and his arm had started bleeding again. With an agitated twist of his wrist, he turned off the faucet.

Enough was enough. He'd let this mushroom way out of proportion. She was just a woman—and barely that. She wasn't even pretty. Well, he amended grudgingly, maybe she was—at least prettier than he wanted to admit. She was softer, too, he conceded, remembering the way her body had felt pressed to his side as they'd stood close together over the sink. And she was more substantial—her commando tactics in his kitchen, a case in point—than he'd given her credit for being. Even Bax had crowed about how she'd toughed out the rigorous day, hawking her virtues like a snake-oil salesman peddling his goods. None of that meant, however, that he had to be so totally and dangerously preoccupied with thoughts of her that he'd damn near gotten himself crippled today.

Determined to put things back in perspective, he made quick work of drying off. Knotting a towel at his hips, he stalked out of the bathroom.

He would not be a slave to testosterone.

He would not pussyfoot around in his own home.

He would not...survive this, he realized dismally as he stopped short in the kitchen door and caught sight of her at the sink.

Except for a flesh-colored lacy scrap of a bra, she was bare to the waist, the porcelain perfection of her skin bathed in the glow of the recessed lighting.

Her head snapped around when she heard his muffled oath.

That soft, maddeningly seductive mouth of hers formed a rounded O of surprise when she saw him standing there. And her eyes, exotic, expressive, as startled as a deer caught in a spotlight, widened then darkened with...with what?

Embarrassment? he wondered, watching her. Maybe. But only for a moment before her small chin came up in a show of defiant pride.

His heart stalled when he saw something else, as well. Something that ran in tandem with his own reactions. That reluctant awareness he knew she'd been fighting. An undeniable arousal that she appeared to be denying with the same annoying lack of success that he was.

The air suddenly grew thick with sexual tension. Too thick to breathe. Too thick to think. A long, humming moment stretched between them as he tried to deal with things that were out of sync, out of time and out of reason for both of them.

She met his eyes and swallowed hard. "I...I'd decided that you..." She stopped, drew in a deep, gut-knotting breath that expanded surprisingly generous breasts—beautiful breasts—that were barely concealed by the sheer fabric of her bra. "I'd decided...that you must have gone to bed."

Breathless now, tentative as she faced him, she abandoned her explanation as her gaze keyed into some startling revelations of her own. Like the fact that he had less clothes on than she did. And that the towel knotted loosely at his hips was slightly tented.

"The...the blood..." she offered lamely as color flooded her cheeks. Her gaze darted from his groin, to his eyes and belatedly to the dripping wet blouse she lifted from the sink where she'd been scrubbing it. "I...I didn't want it to stain..."

Her words trailed off as his blatant arousal and the intimacy consumed them. They were two strangers, yet here they stood, he in nothing but a towel and a scowl, she in a pair of skintight jeans and a scrap of lingerie that revealed more than it concealed. And what it revealed held him spellbound.

The burnished brown circles of her aureoles showed through the sheer fabric. He swallowed hard, as beneath his gaze, the tips of her nipples tightened to small hard peaks. He could visualize holding her shimmering weight in his hands, possessing her velvet softness with his mouth.

He was barely aware that she'd stopped talking. Barely aware that he'd taken several slow, deliberate steps to-

ward her...until she turned away from him. Until she
closed her eyes and lowered her head. Until he realized that
the hand she raised to brush the hair away from her face
and tuck behind her ear was trembling.

The dewy softness of her cheek had flushed to a warm,
dusty rose. The blush disclosed a gentle vulnerability, a
trait she covered well with her in-your-face boldness. A
trait he'd suspected but never confirmed until this moment when it caught her off guard. If he didn't miss his
guess, it was also something she'd never own up to. Instead, she'd deny it as a weakness. Oddly, because she
came on so strong, that insight into her vulnerability
caused a tide of tenderness to lap through him. He was
curious to know what had forced her to grow her prickly
protective shell.

Stronger even than his curiosity, was his awareness of
her seductive femininity. As the silence lengthened and the
sense of intimacy heightened, that awareness teamed
recklessly with desire.

It didn't make any sense, but he couldn't stop looking
at her. And he couldn't look at her without wanting her.
The delicacy of her bare shoulders, fine boned and grace-
ful, drew his gaze and held it. The fragile framework of her
ribs, the slender curve of her waist circled by the snug
waistband of her jeans, invited more than a visual caress.

He clenched his jaw and his fist in tandem to keep himself from reaching for her, aware as he did so that it was
her needs, not his, that took precedence. He wanted her so
badly that if he touched her now he might hurt her.

"I—just let me go grab a sweater," she said in a hushed,
hurried voice that might have convinced him she wasn't as
shaken as he was if she hadn't sounded so breathless.

Spinning away from the sink, she shouldered past him toward the kitchen door. "I'll be right back and dress those wounds for you."

His hand snaked out and grabbed her arm to stop her.

Childlike, vulnerable again and achingly submissive, she stood statue still. He could see the pulse racing at the hollow of her throat. Feel the heat of her blood rise to warm her skin.

Her skin. It was as soft to the touch as its silken sheen had promised. The flesh and bone it covered, more fragile than her brassy independence would ever lay claim to.

Ever so slowly she raised her eyes to his. In question. In confusion. In request.

With the last of the will he possessed, he loosened his hold. Slowly he unwrapped his fingers from around her upper arm. "Go to bed, Kelsey."

The gruffness of his voice was diluted only by the effort it took not to pull her into his arms and pin her against the kitchen wall with his body. To dip his head and taste the pleasure her sensual lips promised. To fill his palms with the delicate weight of her breasts, to fill her body with his pulsing heat and the raging arousal that ruled his thoughts and tested his control.

She blinked, her eyes relaying a long, slow appeal that seemed to say yes and no and at the same time ask, *What's happening here?*

"Your hand—" she finally managed to whisper into a silence so thick, it hurt to breach it.

"Is fine," he gritted out, unflinching in his bid to regain the control her presence threatened and that he came so close to losing.

"Go to bed," he repeated, barely above a whisper. He needed her out of his sight and out of his reach so he could

figure out when he'd gone out of his ever-loving mind.
"Go to bed and stay there."

Go to bed and stay there. It would have been the wise
thing to do, Kelsey admitted as she rummaged around in
her suitcase for something to put on. It would also be the
safe thing to do. She found an oversize jade green sweater,
tugged it over her head and tried to ignore the pulse beating wildly in her ears.

"So when have you ever done anything because it was
wise?" she asked herself aloud. Never. At least not in recent memory. And playing it safe had never factored into
her equations, either.

With hands that she refused to admit were less than
steady, she rummaged through her oversize cosmetic bag.
Finally she came up with the essential oils, herbal tea and
the candle that she wanted.

"It's only eight o'clock at night," she muttered with
righteous justification as she gathered the healing arsenal
in her arms and marched out the bedroom door. "Who
goes to bed at eight o'clock at night?

"And who cries uncle when there's a job to do? Or takes
orders from a man?" she added, building her case for
facing Lucas Caldwell again that night. "Who does he
think he is—my father?"

That thought slowed her steps as she hurried down the
hallway toward the kitchen. Slowed them until she
stopped, closed her eyes and regrouped. One of these days
she would get past the sting. One of these days she would
stop hearing the disapproval in her father's voice, seeing
the disapproval on his face as he tore apart what she'd
done, shamed her into doing it over, into perfecting what
she'd thought was already perfect, undermining her confidence with his constant attacks on her performance.

"Grow up, Gates," she muttered under her breath. "Or give up on trying to please him."

But as she rounded the door and brazened her way into the kitchen, her father became a distant presence in her thoughts. And the look Lucas Caldwell gave her when she walked tentatively into the room, ground into dust any outside notion that when he'd ordered her to bed, the command had held any paternal conviction.

That look was devastating as he stood near the counter watching her. In his broad palm, was a half-full tumbler of shimmering liquor. In his eyes was a spellbinding combination of helplessness and harassment. Disdain and desire. And it took everything she had in her to face him down and accomplish what she'd set out to do.

She had to prove to him that she did not cry uncle. She had to prove to herself that she was the master of her own actions, not him. And certainly she had to prove that this hormonal ambush that had them both as skittish as the new calves Bax had shown her this afternoon, was not going to rule her actions. Proving it had become a point of honor. A mandatory exercise in self-control.

"I thought you went to bed," he said with a weary sort of acceptance. The statement relayed not only his fatigue but the fact that he'd have been more surprised if she'd actually stayed put.

"Well, you see," she said, willing her voice to sound casual and perky in the face of a well-honed self-preservation instinct that begged her to *git while the gittin'* was good, "that's another one of those things that falls under the category of 'there's more to me than meets the eye.' Once I start a job, I finish it."

She nodded toward his hand, determined not to get sidetracked by the sight he made standing there in nothing but his towel and his attitude. A tough trick when everywhere she looked she encountered bare, bronze skin, lean, corded muscle and enough steely tension to support an I-beam. He was a beautiful male machine. Sleekly molded, savagely strong.

He was built broad at the shoulders and lean at the hips, something his workingman's clothes had suggested and his near nudity supported. All muscle. All sinew. All man, from the thick mat of dark chest hair sprinkled sparsely with silver that arrowed and darkened as it disappeared beneath the towel riding low on his hips, to the smooth, triangular build that exemplified substance and strength.

While he'd been gifted with the fluid lines and angular beauty of an athlete, no exclusive men's club gym had molded a body that could have been a substitute for Michelangelo's David. Hard work had honed his physique to the rough-hewn masterpiece it was today. Even the numerous and varied scars riding the plains of his ribs, glancing across the angular curve of his shoulder, or the more recent injuries, still angry and bleeding, enhanced rather than marred his physical appeal.

He was, in short, a hell of a man. A man's man—as well as a woman's. A man a woman would want to call hers. Which had her wondering again about the frilly white bedroom in a house otherwise lacking in feminine touches.

Curiosity blended dangerously with a scorching, insistent desire to know if those dark eyes and that dangerous scowl ever conceded to an emotion more powerful than anger. To a need more demanding than self-preservation.

He tipped the glass to his lips and downed it in one long swallow. She dragged her gaze away, reminding herself that he was a means to an end. No matter how pretty he is, no matter how compelling, she couldn't afford to get involved with this cowboy either physically or emotionally.

Her heartbeat accelerated without warning when she realized that of the two possible entanglements, she wasn't sure which one scared her most, the physical or the emotional. The one thing she was sure of was that either one would be costly.

"Those wounds still need attention," she said, needing to get focused and intending to do just that.

He set the empty tumbler on the counter. "I told you, I'll slap on some Band-Aids. I'll be fine."

"Caldwell," she said, brazening it out with the hope that she'd managed a tolerant, reasonable tone. "You're not going to win this one. Go put on some pants, then get back here and I'll take care of them. No big deal, okay?"

But it was a big deal. A very big deal, she admitted truthfully, as they squared off one more time. Like her, however, he must have decided that for him to balk at this stage of the game would be admitting just how big of a deal it was.

With a deep breath and a long slow blink, he turned and left the room.

Four

It was only after he left the kitchen that Kelsey realized she'd been holding her breath beneath her perky little take-charge smile. She let it out on a whoosh that stirred the hair that had slipped over her eyes.

Lord, the man was intense. And angry. That anger stung more than it should have. It also negated those notions she'd been courting that he was attracted to her.

"Time for a reality check, Gates," she cautioned herself sternly. "I mean, think about it—*really* think about it—and you'll see how absurd it is."

Jonas Gates's feisty daughter had never been the kind of woman who elevated pulse rates and drove men wild with desire. Wild with *anger,* maybe, but her boyish body and Osmond-like wholesome face and smile did not inspire protracted attacks of passion. It seemed unlikely at this stage of the game that a man—especially this man—would succumb to her as-yet-undiscovered siren's lure.

What she'd convinced herself was attraction, in reality was a trick of light and shadows. Just like that provocative tenting of his towel. He was, after all, a big man. It stood to reason he'd be big all over without benefit of provocation.

No, she'd slipped over the edge with the mutual attraction theory. Clearly, he could hardly tolerate her presence. The exhausting undercurrents swirling around them like the wind zipping around a mountain pass computed to animosity not chemistry. And what had been lust at first sight on her part, had been a case of dislike at first sight for him.

She should be used to evil eyes and reluctant subjects by now. It came with the territory. It shouldn't hurt—even a little—that he seemed so intent on disliking her. She'd eat a horseshoe before she'd admit it to him. She was having a hard enough time admitting it to herself. It might not have cut so deep if it wasn't so glaringly obvious that the root of his animosity was a holdover attitude someone else had perpetuated. Possibly some other woman. Probably the one who had decorated that white-on-white bedroom.

So he'd been burned. Who hadn't? she rationalized, tamping down on a surge of compassion. She shouldn't have to bear the brunt of his anger because of someone else's sins. True, he didn't have to like her in order for her to do her job. It would help, though, and because of that she wasn't about to give up. She'd cracked harder cases than Caldwell and the stakes had never been been this high.

Telling herself that the only reason she needed him to like her was for the sake of the story, she shored up her determination to knock down a few of those walls he'd built around himself—walls higher than the Big Horns and thicker than his insufferable head.

She set her armful of oils, the tea, and her candle on a
corner of the table and looked them over. Shoving up her
sweater sleeves and brushing the hair out of her eyes, she
worked hard at nonchalance as she measured out ingredi-
ents for a salve.

That done, she forced a deep, cleansing breath. Feeling
marginally more in control, she set the table and retrieved
both the casserole and the salad Naomi had left for them.
After she set the teakettle on to boil, she lit her candle.

When she heard him enter the kitchen a moment later,
she told herself she was ready for him. And she could
handle it. She'd handled in-the-trenches accounts of the
L.A. riots and the devastation of her own apartment in the
last quake. She'd handled the wrath of both her father and
the LAPD over her report on sexual harassment within the
male-dominated ranks. She could handle one stoic, mean-
tempered cowboy.

She took a deep breath and faced him.

And found her resolve slinking away again.

He'd slipped into soft, fawn-colored moccasins, a pair
of well-lived-in jeans and a loose, collarless chamois-
colored long-sleeved cotton shirt. He'd left the shirttails
out and rolled the cuffs on both arms above the elbow.
Couple this pleasantly rumpled look with damp hair softly
curling at his nape, and the man-of-steel facade trans-
formed before her eyes to a man comfortable in his own
element, yet vulnerable in her presence.

Back up the truck, Gates, she warned herself. *He's
about as vulnerable as one of the monster bulls Bax
showed you today. Just do the deed and get to the story.*

"This won't take long," she promised, shooting for a
businesslike voice as she nodded toward the chair.

In silent and reluctant submission, he walked to the chair and sat. Then brows furrowed, he raised his chin, alert as a cat.

"What the hell is that?" he demanded, sniffing the air.

She quirked a brow, amused, in spite of everything, at his damnable suspicion. "What? This?" She slid the candle toward him.

He leaned closer, sniffed again and frowned. "Roses. It smells like roses."

"Give the man a cigar. Smells good, huh? And relaxing. No? Just give it a chance, then. Rose oil is known for its sedative qualities. In addition, it has antibacterial and astringent benefits. Just breathe in the fragrance. And stretch that arm out, would you?" She poised before him with the little pot of salve she'd just blended.

His hand reached out to snag her wrist before she could administer the dressing.

"It's just petroleum jelly mixed with a few drops of essential oils," she sputtered, answering the question in his scowl and the reticence in his eyes. "Calendula is an herb from the flower. Lavender's another herb. Both have healing powers. Oh, for heaven's sake, give it a rest. I want a story, Caldwell. I'm not about to try to knock off my best source of information just because he's rude, reluctant...and a reeeaaally tolerant man," she added with staged sincerity when his narrow-eyed scowl warned her she was pushing it.

Slowly he relaxed his hold and made a quick, visual inventory of the exotic-looking vials cluttering one corner of the table.

"What is all this stuff?"

The teakettle began to whistle.

"Witchcraft." With a wicked grin, she filled a teapot she'd found on an earlier foray into the cupboard and set the tea to steep. "Aromatherapy," she amended with a laugh when his scowl deepened. The man was as tense as a sky diver on his first jump. For some reason his unease took the edge off of hers.

"Aromatherapy?"

"The art and science of using the essential oils of flowers and herbs for their healing properties. Don't look like that," she scolded, concentrating on the job at hand as she took his hand in hers again. "The method is ages old, tried and true. As a matter of fact, it's been traced back to the ancient Egyptians."

He snorted. "Do I look like an Egyptian?"

She didn't know what surprised her more. The fact that he actually had a sense of humor, that he chose to express it or the spontaneous laugh she couldn't seem to keep from bubbling out.

"What you look like is a little boy trying to talk his way out of a shot. Relax. I was simply trying to impress upon you that aromatherapy is not as off-the-wall as it sounds. It's been making a resurgence lately. None too soon, if you ask me. That's why I made a point to study and learn about it so I can use it."

Now he was regarding her as if he'd decided she might be about one brick shy of a full load. "What does that make you, some kind of a—"

"Nut?" she supplied brightly.

"I wasn't going to say that."

"No, but you wanted to. That assessment aside, however, what it makes me is a believer in natural healing. Just like fear of the unknown makes you a skeptic.

"Think about it," she added when his eyes narrowed in denial. "In a time of synthetic drugs and their unknown long-term effects, a few alternative approaches are in order. Aromatherapy is one of them. It's completely natural and totally beneficial. Now hold still. And just give it a chance. Unless you really are afraid I might hurt you," she baited, playing on his pride.

When he deliberated, then reluctantly held out his arm, she smiled. Interesting, she thought, that it had taken a challenge to finally turn the tide. He wouldn't do it for the sake of helping himself, but he would do it rather than back away from a thrown gauntlet. She stored away that piece of information, figuring it might become useful later.

In the meantime, there were his injuries to consider. Despite his attitude, she wanted to help him. With infinite care, she applied the salve in liberal amounts to the angry, swollen abrasions on the back of his hand, then to the ones on his forearm. By the time she'd finished, she felt a subtle relaxing of his muscles.

She gave him a cautious smile. "It feels better, doesn't it?"

He thought, frowned, flexed his hand, frowned again then drew in a considering breath. "Yeah," he admitted grudgingly. "Maybe."

"It's the cajeput," she offered, satisfied with her victory, no matter how minor. "I added a couple of drops because of its pain-relieving properties. The lavender helps there, too, but it's more of an antiseptic.

"Don't worry," she added, sensing his misgiving mounting instead of receding. "I left my needles at home."

That earned her another narrow-eyed look. "Needles?"

"I'm also a student of acupuncture."

"Oh, brother."

She grinned. "You don't know what you're missing. I could take care of that tension headache you've got in short order. And don't deny that you've got a headache."

She touched a finger to the furrow between his brows. "It's written all over your face."

He grunted his opinion of what he thought of her assessment, but neither admitted to the pain nor disputed her. Another minor concession. Its significance wasn't lost on her.

After rising and drying her hands, she poured them each a cup of tea. When he took a measuring sniff of the mug she set in front of him, she shook her head. "You are the most suspicious man. It's just tea."

"Doesn't smell like tea."

"That's because it's an herbal blend you aren't used to. Rose hip, mint and chamomile. The chamomile will help you relax."

"I don't need to relax. And I don't drink tea."

"Yeah, I know." She took a sip from her own cup. "Cowboys don't drink tea or eat quiche. Tonight, you drink tea. It's part of the healing process. And you *do* need to relax. It also helps you heal."

He tilted his head and considered her for the first time as if he truly didn't know what to make of her. "Are you always this bossy?"

She arched a brow. "Are you always this difficult?"

He drew a deep breath, shook his head, then buried his face in his good hand. "When, exactly did I lose control?"

She sat back, pleasantly surprised, and enjoyed the look of him—the slow, but sure relaxing of muscle, mind and guard. She was beginning to think the tension she'd felt between them from word one had all been a product of her overactive imagination and overstimulated hormones.

"Careful there, Caldwell, you might just smile. That's the second time I've caught you on the brink today."

He raised his head and considered her. "I'm not going to give you an interview."

Her smile faded. Well, score one for reality. It had been pure wishful thinking to hope that his somewhat good-natured grousing had been the beginning stages of a cease-fire between them.

Smoke screen. It had all been an elaborate smoke screen to camouflage deeper doubts and embedded secrets. And, she suspected, to defuse the sexual tension that surprised her when it crept back in.

There she went again. Sensing something that wasn't there. Abetting a notion only she was a party to. Well, the sexual tension she could do without. That and the admiration she was beginning to feel for the way he stuck to his guns.

"I want that interview," she assured him, giving him fair warning that she didn't intend to back down. "And I think it's just a question of wearing you down before I get it. Besides, sooner or later I figure you'll start to feel guilty about palming me off on Bax."

"Yeah," he agreed, studying her determined grin as he landed back in the chair. "I guess that was a little mean-spirited. But I figure Bax will forgive me eventually."

She flashed him a patently manufactured smile. "A joke. How nice. I wouldn't have guessed you had one in you. I think the tea is working. Have some more. We'll talk."

He raised the mug to his lips again. Again he sniffed.

His continued suspicion prompted another laugh. "Guess you'll never really know for sure if I might have put something extra in it, will you? Something guaranteed to loosen your lips and relax your guard. Why is it that you feel you have to play your cards so close to the vest with me, Caldwell?"

He gave her a look that said, *Do you really have to ask?*

"Okay," she conceded and tried a tack that was no less direct. "So I'm a reporter, and that makes me lower than pond scum in some people's books. But I'm actually here to help your cause, not hamper it."

When he remained silent, she set about bandaging his hand and added, "Unless, of course, you really do have something to hide."

She sensed the very slightest tensing of the muscled strength beneath her hands. Whether it was her touch or the directness of her question, something had shifted between them. Like the earth shifts in the throes of a quake. Like the wind shifts in the face of a storm.

One look into his eyes, dark and intense on hers, and she figured she had her answer. At least her body answered, as inside her, something tightened, tautened, then let go in a spiral of heat and need and longing. Something innately physical and undeniably strong.

"I raise cattle." The softness of his voice sent a tingle shimmering through her blood. "What could I possibly have to hide?"

She swallowed hard and tore her gaze away, cursing her female hide for getting caught up again in something that was both futile and foolish. Instinctively aware of his eyes on her as she moved her fingers from his hand to his forearm, she concentrated on keeping her own hands steady. "You tell me. What could it be?"

"You know, Ms. Gates," he said after a long moment, "you have a decidedly nasty habit of answering a question with a question."

She put the finishing touches on the dressing, then risked meeting his eyes again. "Kelsey. Please call me Kelsey. And it's in the genes."

He quirked a dark brow.

"The curiosity, the quiz-'em-'til-they-collapse approach," she explained. "My father is also my employer."

He snorted. "Figures."

"No. It's not what you think. I'm not there because I can't do anything else and Daddy provides a job for his little princess."

Hearing the defensiveness in her tone, she stopped, drew a deep breath and settled herself down. "I'm there because he doesn't want me there. I'm kind of like the proverbial wart on his nose. I don't adhere, so to speak, with his code of journalism. Which, translated means, I write what I want to write, not what he wants me to write.

"But what I *do* write is damn good," she added quickly. "Good enough that he has to put up with me, but not good enough, in his opinion, that I don't have to fight for every inch of space in his precious paper."

He studied her for a long time before finally asking, "So why are you still there?"

She thought about that for a minute. "Mostly just to tick him off, I suppose." And to rub his nose in the fact that I'm his daughter and I can do it my way whether he approves or not. And to prove to him I'm good. To blow his socks off with the biggest story known to God, man and machine and the knowledge that I did it in spite of him, not because of him. To make him love me for who I am, instead of who he wants me to be.

But that was her drama to work through. No one else's. And no one else needed to know about her holdover Freudian foibles.

"So part of the reason you're here is to irritate him."

She met his gaze and lied through her teeth. "I actually do some things for a cause other than my own. It's like I told you. I'm interested in writing an impactful piece on the decline of the American rancher."

"I know what you told me," he said, dismissing her justification for the crock it was. "What I want to know is what are you *really* doing here."

The cowboy didn't pull any punches. And he wasn't buying her story. Which could mean that he was suspicious of her true motives. Did he sense that she was bent on linking him with Harrison Montgomery? Did he even suspect that Montgomery might be his father? And the big question, if he did, would he ever admit it to her?

Donna Caldwell may be the only one who could confirm her suspicions. Unfortunately, Donna Caldwell wasn't here. Lucas was. And Lucas Caldwell was about as eager to talk to her as a condemned man was to walk to the gallows.

The analogy was oddly chilling—and no doubt accountable for the guilt that increased with each passing moment. Now, however—if ever—was not the time to come clean. Not if she wanted to break the story that every instinctive bone in her body told her she'd find here.

"Why is it that you feel you can't believe me?"

"Why would I want to?" he asked, point-blank.

With great effort, she managed not to fidget under his direct gaze. Those golden eyes seemed to stare a hole the size of Wyoming through her deception. They saw too much, because the bare truth was that she wasn't leveling with him. It's your job, she reminded herself, reaching deep for justification.

She forced a smile. "Now who's answering a question with a question?"

He watched her for a silent moment. After a long slow blink and a deep, weary breath that expressed both annoyance and disappointment, he said, "You can blame yourself for that. I've been studying your technique. Once you get the hang of it, it's an easy pattern to fall into.''

As jabs went, it was fairly benign. Considering him over her tea, she decided it was safe to push once more. "*Is* there another story here, Caldwell?''

He let out a tired breath. "No, *Gates*. There is no other story. So if you're here thinking you can fabricate one, you're going to be grossly disappointed.''

She held his gaze for as long as she could. As long as she dared. "Fair enough,'' she said, with a smile that implied the case was closed. "Let's stick with the issue at hand.''

And the issue at hand was to continue chipping away at his reserve until he trusted her enough to let down his guard. The only problem was, every time she thought she was making headway, she got sidetracked by that chemistry thing that insisted on cropping up. Inexperienced as she was in dealing with it, she found herself vacillating again on whether she was making the man's heart throb or giving him a case of heart*burn*.

She had no doubts about her own reactions. She was about to short-circuit from the overload. Even fully clothed, every line and angle of his body and profile was lovingly defined and artfully molded. The dim light and shifting shadows they shared in his kitchen tonight intensified her awareness of the differences between a woman and a man. The longer she spent in his presence, the more difficulty she had fabricating reasons not to give in to the lure of exploring the more pleasurable side of those differences.

"I don't know about you,'' she said, stalling the temptation by grasping at the closest straw, "but I'm starved.''

She busied herself by filling his plate with salad and something that smelled wonderful and looked like a thick beef stew. Then she filled her own plate.

Deciding that risking his wrath over her persistence was preferable to the dangerous drift her thoughts had been taking, she pressed him again. "How about the leased land issue? Proposed legislation could cut deep into your pockets, could it not?"

He brought a forkful of stew to his mouth. "Bax can fill you in."

"Oh, yes . . . Bax." She set down her own fork. "Look. Don't get me wrong. Bax is a sweetheart. But he's already told me more about cross-breeding cattle than I ever want to know, and more stories about the good old days than there *were* good old days. I want to hear it from you."

He drilled her with a look. "No interview. How can I make it any clearer?"

"The election could make quite a difference, couldn't it?" she plodded on, determined to break him down, hoping one carefully lobbed bomb might crack through his armored wall.

She thought for only a second before deciding to put her theory to the test. "If Montgomery gets in as president, his stand on the grazing land issue could really hurt you."

Lord, she hoped she hadn't blown it. She held her breath, watching his face carefully for a sign at the mention of Montgomery's name. Any sign. Anger. Betrayal. Hurt. Those implacable wolf's eyes betrayed nothing.

Slowly, deliberately, he swallowed his mouthful of food, set his fork beside his plate and glared at her. "Exactly what part of 'no' is it that you don't understand?"

Exasperated, she slumped back in her chair. "What I don't understand is why you are so resistant to talking with me. I can help you."

"Did I ask for your help?"

That calm, certain restraint he'd maintained from word one had finally slipped a notch. The volume of his voice had increased ever so slightly.

She hoped to capitalize on this small loss of control. "I can reach hundreds of thousands of readers. I can make them sympathetic to the leased land dilemma."

"Did I ask for your sympathy?"

She felt his irritation and figured she'd hit a nerve. "Did you *ever* ask anybody for anything?"

"Now you're getting the picture." He didn't shout. He didn't have to. His impatience was laced through every distinctly enunciated word, written on his face. "What I need, I get. What needs to be handled, I handle. I don't need your help. I don't need your meddling. And I sure as hell don't need your prying into my life."

She told herself that a cautious woman would know when to quit. Just her luck, she didn't have a cautious cell in her body. "That's how you see it?"

He shook his head. "What other possible way is there to see it? I didn't ask you here. I didn't invite your questions. I didn't ask you to fight my battles in your daddy's newspaper."

It was an intended insult. And a direct hit. She made herself look past it and appealed to his sense of fair play. "What about the others?"

He let out a deep breath and dragged a hand through his hair. "What others?"

"The other ranchers. The ones who are on the brink of going under. The ones who *will* go under if the legislation gets passed."

The grim set of his mouth told her her ploy had worked. Ah, guilt. How well she knew it was a great motivator. He *did* feel some responsibility. Playing on his sense of duty, she pressed even harder. "If Montgomery gets in and he has his way, the grazing fees on not only the Bureau of Land Management land but the federal land will triple in the next ten years and force several people out of business. I can't believe you don't care about what happens to them."

He shot her an incredulous look. "As if you do?"

She managed to look offended. "I wouldn't be here if I didn't."

"Somehow I find that difficult to swallow."

"Okay," she conceded again, something she was getting pretty good at. "You're suspicious. I'll give you that. But all my actions aren't motivated by personal gain. I do care."

Oddly enough, while it hadn't started out that way—just as she hadn't factored in her attraction to Caldwell—she hadn't counted on becoming sympathetic to the rancher's dilemma. Bax was, in part, responsible for changing that. Midway through the day, she'd found herself fighting to keep from getting caught up in the very issue that was intended to be her facade for the meat of her real investigation.

The look on Lucas Caldwell's face, however, told her he wasn't about to accept that she might care about his fellow ranchers.

His cynicism, though not entirely inaccurate, riled her. "Okay, Mr. Overanalytical Cynic. Enlighten me. Why am I here?"

He studied her with narrowed eyes. "I haven't figured that out yet. I don't think you have, either. But I will tell you this. You're going to be disappointed. I have nothing to offer you here. No story. No secrets. No interview."

With that, he shoved away from the table, rose and walked with his dirty dishes to the counter.

"The gentleman doth protest too much, me thinks," she mumbled under her breath half hoping he'd hear her.

He did. "You think whatever you want. Just do your thinking somewhere other than around me."

She stood, gathered her own dishes and joined him by the sink. "Do I really scare you that much?"

He laughed, a low growl that held less humor than it did frustration. "Fear has nothing to do with it."

"Then what does?"

The instant she'd blurted it out, she realized it was a question better left unasked. The look in his eyes said he wanted to answer her. And that she'd pushed him an inch too far.

Her heart beat out a warning. It was too late to retrace her steps and retreat to a safe distance away from him. Too late to undo the fact that she'd backed him into a corner that required either an answer or a demonstration.

Through a haze of anticipation and longing it occurred to her that they were back where this had all started. Side by side by the sink. In the glow of the recessed lighting. Amidst the lingering electricity left over from their first encounter.

And she knew in a heartbeat that what she'd tried to talk herself into as a play of light and shadows had been a stark and gripping reality. His attraction to her was as real and as powerful as the moment and more than a little intimidating.

A new intimacy, more compelling than even that suggested by their near-undressed state earlier, had gone to work. An intimacy implicit with the vastness of a land where the closest neighbor was an hour away and the only chaperon was an aging cowpoke who'd turned out the light in his bunkhouse at sunset. An intimacy magnified by the darkness of night and the constant tick of a clock that represented their only company.

She read the dark look in his eyes for what it was. And this time, there was no mistaking its meaning.

Images of what seemed like a lifetime ago, but in reality was less than an hour, came back to her with vivid clarity. The lean, bare breadth of his muscled chest. The silken softness of the dark springy chest hair brushing against her fingers. The heat of his body and the beat of his heart beneath her hands. The pain and fatigue mixed with hunger. And the way his entire body had tensed, not in repulsion as she'd tried to make herself believe, but in anticipation of her touch.

She swallowed hard and somehow managed to meet his gaze. What she found there stole her breath and the last fragments of denial. It was all there. The hunger. The need. The wanting. More intense than she thought she could handle. More thrilling than anything she could name.

And there was something else. An overpowering determination that told her that this time he wasn't going to walk away.

Five

He was a man who had placed emphasis on doing the right thing all of his life. And he knew he shouldn't touch her. Touching her was exactly the wrong thing to do. Anything to do with her would be wrong.

Amazing, he thought, as he moved without hesitation toward her, how easy she made it to break the pattern.

He was past making excuses for his preoccupation with her. He was past trying to figure out why she had this effect on him. He only knew it had been too long since a woman made him feel this way. Too long to stop the wanting. Too long to deny the need.

He didn't try to tell himself he could have stopped himself from reaching for her. It would have been a lie. He no longer had any choice. The wanting had taken over.

His only solace was his ruthless conviction that wanting her had nothing to do with feelings. Feelings were for dreamers and fools. Once he'd been both. Now he was neither. What this had to do with was sex. Just sex. Raw and real. Stark and demanding.

Steeped in that conclusion, fighting the possibility that something about her had resurrected emotions long dead and buried, he let the burn take over. Let the desire to feel her slender yet lush woman's curves against the hard, lean heat of his body reach flash point.

The ache to feel her long legs, elegantly supple, actively aggressive, entwined with his, consumed him. The need to hear her whispered moans and throaty cries in the dark of night, in the intimacy of his bed, forced a slow, tortured breath to escape through flared nostrils. He reached for her, knowing as he did, the magnitude of the mistake he was about to make.

The look on her face told him she knew it, too. Yet she stood there, the light above the sink heightening the rising flush of color in her cheeks, intensifying the comprehension in her eyes. Green eyes gone soft with invitation, yet glittering with uncertainty. Green eyes a man could get lost in.

He touched the flat of his thumb to her throat as she swallowed. Delving his other hand into the thick, red silk of her hair at her nape, he pulled her near, until the heavy rise and fall of her breasts beneath her sweater brushed his chest.

Soft. She was so soft. So much softer than she wanted him to believe, both physically and emotionally. A woman's softness had been missing from his life for so long. He closed his eyes and savored the pleasure made more intense because of that absence.

Her heat nestled against him, breast to chest, hip to thigh, and with the slightest pressure of his hand at the small of her back, as intimately as if they were making love.

"Caldwell," she whispered, her voice a tentative caress as he knotted his fingers in her hair and slowly tipped her face to his. "Do...do you really think this is...such a good idea?"

"If I was thinking..." His voice sounded gruff, even to his own ears. He swallowed hard and, lowering his head to hers, brushed her mouth with his, taunting, teasing, tempting them both beyond reason. "If I was thinking, this wouldn't be happening."

Somewhere it registered that what he'd said was true. If he was thinking, he'd have hauled his butt out of there and as far away from her as he could get. Australia ought to do it. But rational thought processes had shut down. And the heat and the fragrance drifting from her body in sultry, shimmering waves sucked him in. He moved nearer...to the source, to the flame, to a need he hadn't ever wanted to feel for a woman again.

"What...what about—"

"No more questions," he commanded in a soft growl. "No more talk. I've had a bellyful of both."

She closed her eyes and moaned—a sound laced less with protest than with surrender. Less with hesitation than with need.

"I told you not to come back in here," he reminded her, silencing any possible objection with the touch of his mouth to hers. "I told you to go to bed," he murmured as her lips parted on a sigh beneath his. Shifting his weight, he pinned her against the counter with an intimate, explicit pressure of his hips. "I figure, you came back...you knew what you were liable to get yourself into."

"Yes," she whispered with such open, honest yearning that all he could think about was getting lost in her. In her scent, in her heat, in her mouth that seduced his own surrender with the white-hot drug of desire.

He nipped her full lower lip, tempted by the taste too rich to resist any longer. Too good to believe. Too lush to deny.

He leaned deeper into her body and nudged his arousal against her belly, craving the contact that both eased and intensified the ache.

"Caldwell," she whispered on a reedy little breath filled with so much longing, it gave him no choice but to finally take her sweet, seeking mouth with his own. He kissed her deeply. Possessively. Until he was hopelessly engaged, completely immersed in the melting warmth and satin sleekness he found inside.

She was everything her sassy femininity promised. Electric, untamed energy. Fluid, flowing sexuality as she gave up any token pretense of reluctance and returned his kiss full measure. She pressed her hips and breasts against him, straining to get closer as she came up on her tiptoes and tunneled her hands beneath his shirt.

He lost himself completely then. In each finger stroke she whispered against his bare skin. In the gentle thrust of her breasts against her chest and the feverish sizzle of her skin beneath his hands.

Her mouth. Lord, her mouth. He couldn't get enough of it. And when any sane man would have been satisfied, he went back for more. He took it with a groan, deepening the kiss and the contact with a thoroughness that sent a sensual shiver sluicing through her slim body. A swift and sure awakening. An elemental rush of arousal that had her closing her eyes and catching the breath he'd captured with his own.

She tasted like an angel yet danced her tongue against his with the wickedness of the devil herself. A wild woman. A woman who could take a man to heaven . . . then lead him back to hell on his knees.

The realization was sobering. And head clearing.

This was the very kind of entanglement he'd spent the past ten years avoiding. A woman like her could weaken a man. And a man in his position could not afford to succumb to the temptation. She would promise him everything, play on his weakness, then leave him to deal with his foolishness and the bitter pain of regret that no amount of time could erase.

He saw it all clearly then. While it was a cinch he wasn't in control, it was increasingly obvious that she was.

This was exactly what she wanted from him. To break down his resistance, to inch her way into his trust so she could bleed him dry of integrity, strip him of his pride. Sex led to intimacy. Intimacy to shared secrets. And some secrets he couldn't afford to share with anyone. Especially not with her. A woman who could expose his secrets to the world.

Hell, what had he been thinking? He never should have let this get started. And he damn sure couldn't let it go on. On an indrawn breath, he broke the kiss and wrenched himself away from her. Away from the gentle yielding of her body, the promise of erotic pleasure and the temptation that had lured him in so deep.

While he damned himself for letting it go as far as it had, he channeled his anger at her. "So how was it? Kissing the cowboy everything you'd hoped for?"

She looked dazed. Dazed and aroused and confused.

Her lips were swollen from his kisses. Her eyes hazy and fever bright. When she focused and saw the hard, closed mask he'd drawn across his face, she looked physically bruised. He swore, a concise, crude indictment of his opinion of her methods. He steeled himself against believing anything could hurt her.

"Stay out of my way, city girl," he warned, explicitly reducing what had just happened between them to something calculating and cold. "Or next time, you might get what you came for.

"That was part of the ploy, right? That's what those dewy little doe-eyed looks were all about?" he added when she just swallowed and stared in silence. "A little midnight ride in exchange for a hot story isn't much of a compromise, is it?"

She shrank back against the counter as if he'd struck her.

"I'll have to hand it to you. You've got that wounded look down pat." He refused to be affected by the pain in her eyes. "I'm sure it works well for you. Not this time. This time you picked the wrong approach. Just like you picked the wrong man—for your story and your kicks."

Ignoring her stricken look, he stalked across the kitchen, then stopped in the doorway. He turned back to her with a weariness born of his disgust. "Do us both a favor. Go back to L.A. where you belong. Go back to L.A.—and leave me the hell alone."

Even before she dragged herself out of a bed rumpled from a sleepless night, Kelsey knew that Caldwell was gone. The man had developed a definite pattern of running out on her. In light of his parting words last night, it was a given that he'd make damn sure their paths didn't cross today.

After dressing and groggily making her way to the kitchen to brew some tea, she'd decided she wasn't even disappointed that he'd made another great escape. She needed some distance, too. She was still numb. Just as she'd been numb when he'd left her last night. Numb, aroused and cut to the quick.

She'd stood alone for a long time after he'd stalked out, too taken by storm to dissect what had happened between them. Never had she been hit with so many emotions so fast, so hard and so strong. She'd known the man less than a week and most of that time had been spent either bickering with him or watching his tight backside exit stage left.

Sitting in his kitchen, in the stark, clear light of the morning after, she still felt as trembly as she had last night. She touched a finger to lips that were still swollen and sensitive from the bruising urgency of his kiss. Her heartbeat picked up at the memory. Of his taste. Of his need. Of his swift and angry withdrawal.

It had all happened so fast. It had all ended too soon.

A soft rapping brought her back to the morning and to her senses. Damned if she hadn't been mooning over that cold-blooded cowpuncher. She hated herself for letting him get to her. She'd like to hate him, too, but settled for the hope that his hand and arm ached like thunder—then in the next breath worried that he'd have sense enough to keep the bandages clean.

A second persistent rap had her snapping her head around and tuning in to the fact that someone was knocking on the kitchen door. Frowning, she dragged the hair out of her eyes, walked across the room and swung open the door.

Bax stood on the other side, his battered hat in his hands. "Mornin'," he said, nodding his head like a chicken pecking in the dust. "Lukey says I'm to help with your bags."

Lukey. An endearment out of step with the hard, angry man who'd all but accused her of prostituting herself for a story. The nickname implied soft edges. That Lucas had once been a small, vulnerable child. And that there was a quality about him that made a wizened old cowpoke like

Bax regard him with affection. It hurt, more than she cared to admit, that Caldwell couldn't find it in him to give her a reason to see that side.

"*Lukey*," she said with a bitterness spurred by the brittle memory of his parting shot last night, "seems to want me out of his hair."

Bax's sheepish grin returned along with a shrug of apology. "Yes, ma'am. I b'lieve you could say that's a fact."

Even though she was weary of battling her conflicting emotions where Caldwell was concerned, she couldn't help but answer Bax's grin. "Had your coffee yet, Bax?"

"Yes, ma'am. Had a potful. Reckon I might have room for one more cup, though, specially if Naomi made a pan full of them cinnamon rolls she usually bakes on Wednesdays."

"Well, I *reckon* you know Naomi's routine pretty well." She shot the old cowhand a full-fledged smile. "Come on in. Let's see how big a dent we can make in it."

"Who'd a thought a little thing like you could polish off two of Naomi's gut busters?" Bax pronounced, a little in awe, a lot in admiration, after they'd accomplished what they'd set out to do. He patted his full stomach and sighed.

"I've got this high-tech metabolism," she confided, eyeing another roll but deciding against it. "Keeps me thin and makes women hate me because I can eat anything I want. Oh, well," she added with a one-shoulder shrug. "Thin's still in. And I never set out to win any popularity contests. Your boss is a case in point."

Bax chuckled. "He's a case, all right. A hard case. 'Specially where women are concerned."

She didn't want to be curious about Caldwell's views on women, but damn her female hide, she was. "Care to elaborate on that for me?"

"No, ma'am," Bax said, sounding firm if not tempted. "No, I don't. Figure Lukey's the one to fill you in on anything he wants you to know."

She gave an unladylike snort. "The only thing he wants me to know is the way out of Dodge."

"Oh, now. That's just his way. Don't take it personal."

Just like that kiss last night wasn't personal, she mused, as the memory prompted a simmering heat to streak like quicksilver from her breasts to her belly.

"I reckon he figures he's just protecting what's important to him."

Well, she couldn't argue with that, she thought dismally. She was a threat to whatever secret he was protecting, and he was smart enough to realize it. She dropped her chin into her palm and stared glumly at her empty plate.

Bax fidgeted in his chair, chewed on the wisdom of filling the dreary silence. Finally he let out a deep sigh. "Truth to tell, I think it's his peace of mind he figures needs the most protection."

She thought of Caldwell's brooding scowl and closed-mouthed silence. "He doesn't strike me as having much peace of mind to start with. He's as miserable as a lion with a thorn in its paw."

"I suppose that might be true enough. Mostly though, he's pretty even-tempered and easy to get along with. You ain't seen much a that side of him since you been here though, have ya?" He scratched his jaw thoughtfully. "Can't say what it is about you exactly that sets him off. You ain't nothing like the other one."

She raised a brow, alert suddenly to a puzzle piece just out of her grasp. "The *other* one?"

Bax covered his face with a long, bony hand and eyed her from between spread fingers. "Damnation, I got a mouth on me."

"What other one, Bax?" she insisted, sitting up straighter in her chair. "Are you saying there's a woman in the unbendable Lucas Caldwell's life?" The swift but undeniable distress that the occupant of the white bedroom might still be a factor, stunned her.

"Was," Bax clarified after mumbling under his breath that since he'd already let the cat's tail out of the bag, he'd just as well let the critter loose. "*Was* a woman. But they've been divorced now for pert near ten years. She was from the city, too, but like I said, Elise weren't nothing like you."

Kelsey stared past Bax, absorbing that little tidbit of information. The relief came first. A relief she didn't care to admit to but, like the jealousy, couldn't deny no matter how hard she struggled to discount it. Sometime during the night she'd come to fully embrace her theory that a woman had burned him good. Bax had just confirmed it.

"I don't think it's Elise that he misses so much as it is the boy," Bax mused, almost to himself.

She snapped her gaze to Bax, all senses on red alert.

"The boy?" she echoed, hearing a breathless disbelief in her voice as her heartbeat escalated. "Lucas has a son?"

The legs of Bax's chair scraped against the floor as he shot to his feet. He swore softly then sent her a pathetically trapped look. "It'd be best if we just get them bags in your car so's I can get back to work," he said, clearly uncomfortable with what he'd revealed, "being Lukey figures you'll be gone when he gets back tonight and all."

His rheumy old eyes begged her not to ask him any more questions. Shock, as much as anything else, kept her silent.

A son. Lucas has a son. A son he misses. A sad irony ricocheted around in her head like radio waves bouncing off a satellite. *Like father, like son.* Caldwell didn't see his father. Neither did he see his son. It was too much, suddenly, to absorb. Too many thoughts, too many speculations. For her own peace of mind as much as for Bax, she didn't press him.

"Too bad about you leavin'," Bax added, looking relieved when she didn't ask any more questions. "Kinda liked the idea of being in that story you were writin'. Kinda liked seein' that fire back in Lukey's eyes whenever your name come up, too."

She considered him with a vacant kind of curiosity, still sorting out the news of Lucas's ex-wife and son while wondering where this conversation was actually leading.

"Ain't seen this much of a spark in the boy since he was a young buck feeling his oats. He's a lot to handle when he gets this way." He paused dramatically, then ambled in his bow-legged gait to the door and made sure he had her attention. "Yup. It's a shame you ain't up to the challenge. But then I understand, and all, why you figure you gotta hightail it outta here."

While it took a while to register, it didn't take a market analyst to figure out what Bax was up to. He was baiting her—daring her to stay. The question was, Why? The bigger question was, Did she dare snap at the bait?

Caldwell had made it clear what he thought of her. He'd as much as accused her of prostituting herself for the sake of a story. He thought her the lowest kind of life-form. He wanted her gone.

For the first time since she'd latched on to this story, she wondered if maybe it would be best for all concerned if she gave him what he wanted. It was beginning to look as though she were butting her head against a brick wall anyway, and exercises in futility weren't exactly high on her top-ten list.

Ed would say that if she knew what was good for her, she'd oblige Caldwell and leave. Pack her bags, zip down the lane and out of his life. Forget the story. Forget the ex-wife, the little boy. Forget the way her blood boiled and her breasts ached when she thought of him touching her.

Trouble was, doing what was good for her went against the grain. She sighed deeply. Maybe it was high time to rectify that situation. And maybe it was time to leave Caldwell alone and her own emotional equilibrium intact. Clearly, if she stayed much longer, more than her professional integrity would be sullied. Even after he'd blasted her verbally last night, just remembering what his kiss had done to her had her thinking things and feeling things—man/woman things—that she was at a loss to understand.

By the door, Bax watched her with a subdued expectancy. *Get out while the gittin's good,* a little voice warned her. *Get out before you get in too deep.*

In a resigned silence, ignoring Bax's hangdog look, she headed for the bedroom and dug her bags out of the closet.

Lucas worked the sweaty leather glove carefully off his swollen hand. With a slow, painful flexing of his fingers, he rode out the worst of the ache, tucked his gloves in his hip pocket and headed for the house.

It had been a bitch of a day—following a bitch of a night. He had one mercenary redhead to blame for that. Thanks to her, he'd been in a foul mood from word one.

Unfortunately, the bulk of that mood had been spent on poor Toby Wheeler. He'd lost his temper with Jack Wheeler's fifteen-year-old kid over a stupid thing like overhaying the cattle.

He was a kid for pity's sake. And times being what they were, Toby needed the money his part-time work on the Triple C netted him. What he didn't need was a mean-tempered straw boss chewing a strip off his backside over a minor misjudgment.

He lifted his hat, ran a hand through his hair and promised himself he'd make it up to Toby tomorrow. He should have set things right today. Only, today his black mood had darkened with every hour that passed. That was because every hour that passed, he'd found himself thinking of her.

Damn woman. Damn waspish little redhead. With her green eyes that smiled and teased. With her sweet lush mouth that promised a rich, intoxicating indulgence, then delivered with a mind-bending reality that exceeded his wildest expectations. With her lithe, supple body that nestled and molded and invited the most carnal kind of possession. All for a price. One he couldn't afford.

"Damn her," he swore under his breath as he climbed the back porch steps. He hadn't asked her here. He hadn't invited her to barrel into his life like a wild mustang and tempt him into thinking about taming her.

She wasn't the gentling kind. Hell. She wasn't *his* kind. And, he told himself as he opened the back door, he was glad she was gone. Whatever she'd been up to had been no good. He didn't need her snooping around in his life. And he didn't need her messing around in his head.

Last night was proof of that. He'd tried to deny the attraction but it had proven stronger than his will to keep his distance. Like a storm racing over the mountains, it had come on too hard, too fast. Another day or two with her near and he'd have made them both sorry she'd ever set foot on his land. He would have either ended up using her or throttling her. Neither would have made him proud.

Satisfied maybe, he thought with brutal honesty, but not proud.

Telling himself he wanted nothing more than a hot shower and a filling meal before he headed out for the Cattleman's Association meeting in Sheridan, he slipped into the kitchen and hung his Resistol on the rack.

He'd gotten so used to seeing her gray Stetson hanging beside it, that the significance of its presence there didn't connect at first. When it did a second later, a sweetly erotic scent registered on its heels.

Roses. Roses and mint . . . and something else. Chamomile, she'd called it.

Witchcraft, he called it, and damned her again.

He closed his eyes. Even after she was gone, she haunted him. Made his heart race. Made his blood heat. Made him wish he'd taken her last night when she'd been willing and he'd been half out of his mind with wanting her.

"Rough day?"

His eyes snapped open. He spun around . . . and found himself staring into the sassiest green eyes he'd ever seen. Eyes that smiled warily and seduced a groan from him that he refused to believe held anything but anger.

"What the hell are you doing here?"

She brazened out a smile. "Nice to see you, too, Caldwell. How's the hand?"

He drew a deep, controlling breath and ignored her greeting and her question. "I thought we agreed you were leaving."

She leaned a hip against the kitchen counter and regarded him with congenial defiance. "You might have agreed, but I don't recall being a party to that decision."

"What exactly *do* you agree to—if anything?" he muttered, his jaw clenched in exasperation.

"To do exactly what I told you. Once I start something, I finish it. I'm not finished here yet, Caldwell. I still haven't got my story."

"Oh, right." He sighed heavily, acknowledging the weariness of the day closing in, and a weakness in her presence that he hated himself for feeling. "Your story. How could I have forgotten?"

She eyed him with an odd mixture of hesitation and regret. "Look. I think we ought to talk about last night."

He hung his hands on his hips, tipped his head to the ceiling and muttered a dark oath.

"I don't know why that happened any more than you do," she began in a voice so soft, he hardly recognized it as hers. "But I want you to know, I don't make a habit of coming on to men I hardly know. No matter how badly I want a story, I'd never resort to that tactic. Number one, I don't consider it ethical. Number two, I don't consider what I have to offer that much of a bargaining tool."

He looked at her then and saw, incredibly, that she was serious. She really didn't recognize the gut-knotting, groin-tightening extent of her physical appeal. Amazing. Absolutely amazing. If he'd been thinking with his head instead of his hormones last night, he'd have realized it then. Instead, he'd been a complete and total bastard.

"But I do have something else to bargain with."

His eyes narrowed.

"You want to get rid of me, don't you?"

He swallowed and looked past her, praying his words held more conviction than he felt. "Is the sky blue?"

He sensed, rather than saw her flinch before she gathered herself. She crossed her arms beneath her breasts in an unconsciously protective gesture.

"Then I'll make you a deal," she said, jutting out her chin in what he was coming to recognize as a self-defense mechanism.

"A deal?" he repeated, amazed at how she just kept charging back in his face. "You're on my turf, playing by my rules, and you want to cut a deal? Lady, you just don't know when to quit, do you?"

She smiled. That sweet, secret smile that had lured him toward her in the first place. "Would you believe you're not the first person to suggest that possibility?"

When he just scowled at her, she went on. "Okay. The deal is, we both forget about last night. Chalk it up to tension, fatigue...I don't know—the wrong sign of the moon?" she suggested with a dismissive wave of her hand. "Whatever. The bottom line is, we forget it happened and get on with the business at hand."

"Which business might that be? Me getting on with mine or you getting on back to L.A.?"

She met his eyes with a brassy self-assurance that should have prompted anger instead of bewildered admiration. "The business of the interview. That's all I want. Give me the interview and I'll get out of your hair."

He must be going nuts. He was tempted to say yes. As a matter of fact, the longer he stood there, trying to read her mind behind those glittering eyes, the greater the temptation grew. She was offering him an out. Granted, she'd twisted it around until it was to her advantage, but it was an out, nonetheless. She got what she wanted—at least as much as he chose to give her—and in the bargain, he got what he wanted. Her absence. Which was becoming increasingly critical to his peace of mind.

"It's the only way," she assured him, seeming to sense an impending victory. "I know enough about you to know you're too much of a gentleman to physically throw me out."

He shook his head. She called him a gentleman after he'd been a bastard to her last night. Hell, he was a regular prince of a guy. Just ask Toby.

"And I know Bax well enough to know that even if you tried it, he'd never let you get by with it," she went on.

That much was true. "You've got that old coot eating out of your hand, haven't you?" he said, beginning to taste the bitterness of defeat that was becoming all too familiar.

Her smile was full of affection. "Yeah, well, I'm kind of partial to him, too. Just like you are. I'd never hurt him, Lucas."

The sincerity of her words touched him where he hadn't allowed himself to be touched in a very long time. He didn't want to, but he believed her. Which implied that for some reason he wanted to trust her. *About as damn far as he could throw her,* he reminded himself, trying to crush that notion.

"Two days. Three max," she wheedled with that practiced charm that both mellowed and riled him at the same time. "Then I'll be out of your way and out of your life."

Out of his way? Maybe. Out of his life? Not likely. Not anytime soon.

He stared at her long and hard, damning himself even as his mouth formed the words he knew he'd end up regretting.

"Two days," he stated firmly, giving up and giving in.

A victory grin crept up one side of her smart, sexy mouth. "Starting tomorrow, then."

"Starting tonight," he amended with finality. "You want information on the leased land issue? There's a Cattleman's Association meeting at eight. What you can't find out there isn't worth knowing. Be ready by seven if you want to go." Then he stalked out of the kitchen and hit the shower.

"Forty-eight hours," he told himself, repeating it as if it were a mantra that would get him through this with his sanity intact. "Forty-eight hours and she'll be gone."

Gone. The word reverberated through his mind, suggesting a finality that should have pleased him. He refused to ask himself why it only set him on a sharper edge.

Six

Kelsey was ready and waiting when Lucas stepped into the living room, showing her yet another physical side of his appearance. A side that, like the others, threw her off-balance again.

No working rancher met her this time. No faded jeans. No blue chambray shirt. No soft worn moccasins. Instead, a Wyoming cattleman joined her in a white shirt, dark tie, black suit pants and dress boots. This was a businessman successful at what he did and comfortable in his element. A man who could hold his own in a corporate boardroom or seduce the most sophisticated socialite into a bedroom.

As they silently shared the meal Naomi had left for them, Kelsey wasn't entirely sure she was comfortable with this side of Lucas Caldwell. Not that she was comfortable with any of the sides she'd seen to date. She was just more familiar with them.

Thanks to Bax. Once she'd made up her mind to stay, she'd locked on to Bax like a burr in a mare's tail. She smiled softly, recalling his words with affection and thought of their day together.

After a number of heroic standoffs, Bax had finally frowned, scratched his head and pinned her with a look. "He'll have my hide—worthless as it is—if he finds out I've been yapping my jaws to you."

"Just tell me about it, Bax," she'd coaxed softly and before she could stop herself, made him a promise. "I promise you I'm not out to hurt Lucas."

Liar, her conscious had taunted, reminding her that she had a history of using extreme methods to get her story. It was at that point that she'd discovered she didn't much like the way she'd been seeing herself lately. Wasn't too sure she even liked the woman she'd become—a woman who would charm information out of a well-intended old cowhand who had a weak spot for a young woman and a soft spot for a hard man.

She'd like to blame her father for the driven, succeed-at-all-costs overachiever she'd become. And she'd like to blame Caldwell for this brutal self-assessment. He'd bruised her with his hostile accusations. Stripped her bare with his searing looks and blistering kisses that made her think like a woman instead of a professional.

She'd had to force herself to remember that she had a job to do. In the end, she hadn't gotten much else out of Bax, though. She hadn't really tried. She'd told herself it wasn't because she felt guilty. It was just that she didn't need to be a mathematician to add two and two together and come up with a bad marriage and a manipulative woman—a *city* woman—who'd thought she could civilize a cowboy who liked his life just fine the way it was.

No wonder Caldwell wanted to hate her. No wonder he was so angry with himself that he'd let her get under his skin. And she *had* gotten under his skin. If that kiss he'd given her last night didn't prove it, she didn't know what did. The man had a need. A big one. And buried beneath that anger, the need went deeper than sex. He needed a woman. A good one. One who could shore him up, make him whole and heal the wounds another kind of woman had left in her wake.

Well, that woman sure as the world wasn't her. Not a self-professed mercenary who would sell her soul—but not her heart—for a story. The same mercenary who had lost the heart for prying out any more secrets from Bax after he'd told her that the boy, Cody, was almost eleven years old, and that the last time Caldwell's ex-wife had allowed Lucas to see him—which was a good five years ago close as Bax could figure—Cody was the spitting image of his daddy.

Like father like son, she thought again bleakly, as she watched Caldwell slip into a Western-cut suit coat, hiding a wince as he bumped his injured arm. His likeness to Montgomery was too close to discount, cementing her conviction more than ever that Lucas was Montgomery's son.

The same tragic thought that had gripped her when Bax had told her about Cody clawed at her again as she watched Caldwell. Did it run in the family that the young men related to Montgomery were destined to grow up without their fathers to guide them?

Then as now, she'd felt her defenses slip away and the beginnings of a bone-deep ache of sorrow take their place. A sorrow she didn't want to feel for a man who'd done his damnedest to convince her that her feelings would be wasted on him.

The frail fingers of sympathy wrapped a little tighter around her chest as they left the house together. Walking beside him, aware of his quiet strength, his silent pain, she wondered what kind of a woman would keep a son from his father. And she wondered if this was history repeating itself. Like Cody's mother, Elise, was it Donna Caldwell who was responsible for keeping Harrison Montgomery and Lucas apart? Or was it that Montgomery refused to claim his child as she'd originally conjectured?

If Lucas was Montgomery's son, she reminded herself as they rode in strained silence to Sheridan. She'd bet her daddy's fortune on her theory even though she still didn't have a speck of solid evidence to build on. Nor did she have a clue as to whether Lucas was hiding the connection from her or if he himself was unaware of it.

She watched the rolling landscape drift by and sighed deeply. She didn't want to lose her edge on this story. Yet the deeper she became involved with Caldwell and his past, the harder it became to maintain her enthusiasm.

Besides, even though she'd decided to stay and keep trying, it still looked as if she might never find out. Since Lucas wasn't about to talk, Donna Caldwell was the key, and she was conveniently out of reach. If Lucas had his way, when Donna returned a couple of days from now, Kelsey would be nothing more than a bad memory.

For the first time since she'd begun this quest, she seriously entertained the notion that maybe it would be best to end it that way.

"We think he'd make an excellent state representative," Sharon Russell confided to Kelsey over coffee and homemade brownies after the business meeting had adjourned. "Nate's been after him for years. But Lucas is stubborn. And determined to stay out of the public eye. He refuses to run for office even though the Cattleman's Association would back him to the hilt with both monetary and political support.''

Kelsey was working on her fourth brownie and her fourth source of information. The similarities were worth noting. Each brownie was delicious to the point of decadence. Each glowing endorsement of Lucas Caldwell maintained the same theme. His quiet, competent bearing, which she'd admiringly witnessed as he'd conducted the meeting, conveyed a sense of confidence. His sincerity inspired trust and an unimpeachable loyalty that politicians would clamor to purchase by the gross if it could be bottled and sold.

''Why do you suppose that is?'' Kelsey asked Sharon, who, along with her husband, Nate, seemed to act as the unofficial host and hostess of the social hour following the meeting.

Kelsey had liked Sharon upon being introduced to her. Petite, stout and unashamedly graying, she was comfortable with herself and a way of life she didn't want to lose to government intervention. Her enthusiasm for her cause and for Lucas's abilities was infectious. And her opinion was one Kelsey instinctively valued because of her openness and lack of pretension. Sharon personified the overall impression she'd formed of the people who made their living off the land surrounding the Big Horns. She'd found herself developing as much of a fondness for them as she had for the mountains, the wide-open spaces and crisp clean air.

As a side benefit, attending the meeting tonight had given her unexpected insights on exactly what the increase in grazing fees on the federal land would mean. It really could break several good men. And she was beginning to care. Meeting many of them tonight, listening to their concerns, had drawn out a reluctant militance in her toward their cause. The story she'd developed as a cover had begun to gain real significance.

"Why do I think he's so stubborn?" Sharon repeated, cutting into Kelsey's introspective thoughts with a twinkle in her soft brown eyes. "Or why do I think he wants to stay out of the public eye?"

Kelsey shrugged. "Both."

"He's stubborn because it runs in the blood. His grandfather, Nathaniel Caldwell used to set down roots deeper than a sequoia when he made a stand on an issue. Until the day he died, that man was as unbendable as a fence post if he believed he was right.

"As to why he shies away from the public eye . . . I suspect he's just a very private man."

Or, he doesn't want the press to make the connection between him and Montgomery that media coverage would be sure to expose, Kelsey speculated with a frown. Their pictures couldn't run nationally for too long before someone else would pick up on the physical similarities, add two and two together and come up with a whopping four—just the way she had.

Her attention strayed from Sharon to Lucas, where he stood across the room. He was deep in conversation with a group of men who were hanging on his every word as if he were rewriting the preamble to the Constitution.

While most of the ranchers present—both the younger second generation and the seasoned veterans like Nate Russell—were big men in stature, Lucas still overshadowed them. Not necessarily in size, but in bearing. It wasn't that he was demonstrative. Instead, he was soft-spoken and, as she'd witnessed throughout the night, offered his opinions only when prompted. Even then it was with a careful attention to understatement. A natural leader. Like his father, she speculated, thinking of Montgomery's charismatic charm.

She frowned as she watched him, angry suddenly that she wasn't privy to the secrets that brought about the softening in those wolf's eyes of his. Instead, the hard edge of suspicion and disdain were all he was willing to give her. And to "put up with her" until she was out of his hair.

"Quite a man, isn't he?"

She snapped her head around. Sharon was watching her with a look that drew too many conclusions.

Kelsey cleared her throat and straightened her shoulders, intending to nip those thoughts in the bud. "If you go for the strong, silent, rude, brooding and boorish type, I suppose some would find him marginally attractive."

Sharon grinned. "You might be fooling yourself, child, but you have to get up pretty early to fool a Russell. It's all right, you know," she added when Kelsey's eyes narrowed. "You're not the first to knuckle under to the Caldwell charm."

"Charm?" she echoed incredulously when Lucas glanced across the room and spotted her. As if on cue, the softness flirting about the corners of his mouth hardened to steel.

Tearing her gaze away from his, she pasted on her best pretend smile to hide the hurt his antagonism prompted. "Lucas Caldwell has about as much charm as tire iron." She grabbed another brownie, suddenly wanting to talk about anything but him. "These are delicious. Did you bake them?"

Sharon tilted her head in amused speculation. "So what's the story with you two, anyway?" she asked refusing to take the hint to change the subject.

"Story? There's no story," Kelsey insisted, trying to talk around a mouthful of chocolate and wondering why it felt as if she were choking on a lie. "Other than the one I'm writing on the leased land issue."

"Okay. Have it your way. You're not interested in him and he's not interested in you. And George Jones doesn't sing country."

Kelsey frowned, considered this new and unlikely source of friendship and gave it up. Sharon was right. Without her permission and without her knowing it, she'd gone and gotten herself involved with Lucas Caldwell. What a joke. She had the cream of L.A.'s society elite tripping over their feet to woo her and her daddy's money—and she'd fallen for a meanspirited loner who'd rather take a bullet than endure her company. His animosity stung. It hurt even more to have to admit it.

"I just came here for a story," she muttered, and unfortunately, heard more admission in her statement than denial. Sharon heard it, too.

"Well, it happens that way sometimes," Sharon said sympathetically.

"It doesn't happen to me." Hearing the panic in her voice, she settled herself down. "At least it never has."

"Maybe that's because you've never met a man like Lucas Caldwell before."

"Thanks be for small favors." She let out her breath on a long, slow sigh, finally giving up on her protests for the lies that they were. "I must be out of my mind," she confessed dismally.

"Oh, I don't know," Sharon said, considering. "I can't see a lot to want for in a man like him."

She snorted. "Except, maybe, that he regards me as something other than the equivalent of toxic waste."

Sharon laughed. "You sure that's how he feels about you?"

"Trust me, I'm sure. There's only one thing Caldwell wants from me. To see me gone."

"Hmm," Sharon said, her gaze straying to Lucas again. "I wonder why it is then, that when he thinks you're not looking, he's tracking every move you make."

"Probably afraid I'm going to steal something," she grumbled with a dark scowl and knuckled under to another twinge of self-pity.

"He has reason to be wary," Sharon said softly. "It'll take some backbone to weather the storm until he decides to let that wariness go."

Kelsey had no doubt Sharon was referring to Elise. She was beginning to actively despise that woman. For the hard man she'd made of Caldwell. For the barrier she'd left in her wake.

Above all, though, she was beginning to hate herself for losing her focus. Nothing was going the way she'd planned it. She was supposed to be a professional, and here she was, proving her father right by allowing herself to get sidetracked by emotions instead of motive. What difference did it make what Caldwell thought of her anyway? In the end only one thing really mattered: the story. She couldn't afford to blow the biggest one of her career. She needed the recognition it would bring. She needed to rub her father's nose in her victory so she could be free once and for all of the diminished sense of self-worth he'd saddled her with.

What she didn't need was to fall in love.

Love? The thought stopped her cold. She felt the blood drain from her face and her heart roll into a double pump of protest. Love was not an issue here. Lust. Lust was the extent of the involvement she had with Caldwell, and even that was bad enough.

Bad enough to have her reaching for another brownie. Bad enough to have her pulse thundering in denial. Bad enough to make her as cranky as a certain cowboy named Caldwell.

She was as unnaturally quiet on the ride back to the ranch as she had been on the ride into town. Lucas didn't know whether to be thankful or suspicious.

It made him edgy. *She* made him edgy. The unauthorized sense of pride he'd felt as he'd watched her mix in and charm his friends at the meeting had sent him into a rare panic.

And now, alone with her again with nothing but the night and his imagination to run interference, an electric jolt of awareness enveloped him again. He could still taste the sweetness of the kiss he'd taken last night. Still feel the silken heat of her body pressed to his. And he still ached to take her like a man takes a woman and in the process give them both something good.

Only, he didn't have any reason to believe anything good would ever come of an encounter with Kelsey Gates. She was the worst kind of threat to the peace of mind he'd spent the past ten years building. Worse than threatening that peace, though was another unalterable fact. She was a reporter. Every suspicious bone in his body warned him she wasn't leveling with him about her true reason for being here. The leased land issue was a front. If she succeeded in uncovering what he suspected she was really after—a secret, that for his own reason he'd guarded all of his adult life—the damage she could do with the information would be devastating.

He tightened his grip on the pickup's steering wheel and angled his shoulder a little closer to the door—and away from her and the physical tug he'd been battling since he first set eyes on her. Her scent, seductively erotic, yet innocently pure, permeated the cab of the track. It wrapped him in her essence, shaded his perspective and undermined his determination to keep his distance.

But for the full moon and the narrow ribbon of light his headlights splashed across the highway, the evening was midnight black and springtime cool. When he noticed her tugging her lightweight jacket tighter around her, he realized how cool.

He leaned forward and turned up the heater.

"You don't have to do that for me," she announced, sounding testy.

His brows drew together in a frown. "Suit yourself." He reached for the switch and turned it down again.

Several more miles passed with nothing but the soft hum of the radio breaking the tense and expectant silence. He couldn't shake the feeling that like a storm rolling over the mountains gathering force and speed, Kelsey, likewise, was winding up to let 'er rip.

When he sensed her shivering beside him, he scowled and angled her a look.

"Is this some ritualistic exercise in self-restraint, or do you simply enjoy the sound of your own teeth rattling?" he asked, wishing he could ignore her, yet puzzled over what this part of the game was all about.

"Just trying to confine my presence to something you can tolerate," she said crisply, turning her face to the passenger window. "If you're comfortable riding in a rolling meat locker, far be it from me to tamper with your environment."

He worked his jaw and counted to ten. He'd seen her brassy. He'd seen her bossy. At the meeting, he'd even seen her charming a smile from a stone-faced cattle buyer from Buffalo. But he'd never seen her in a snit. It didn't suit her any better than her jacket suited the chilly night. "Too much chocolate make you cranky, does it?"

She mumbled something under her breath, still glaring out the window.

"I didn't catch that."

She turned to face him then. "Too much hostility."

That came out loud and clear. At the same time, it came to him that she was right and that it bothered him that he had been treating her with such cool disdain. Under different circumstances, he might have been compelled to apologize.

He couldn't afford to be bothered. Neither could he afford to apologize. Or to be affected by the hurt in her eyes that she tried to hide with anger. He chose the same course, only he used the anger to cover up the fact that he felt like a heel.

"Look, Gates..." He turned on the heat and sliced her a look that said that particular subject was closed. "I agreed to let you stay on to get your interview. I brought you with me to the meeting and introduced you around. If you're out of sorts because you didn't get the information you needed, don't take it out on me."

"That is so rich," she drawled out with a harsh little laugh. "You're telling me not to take *my* frustration out on you when *you're* the one taking yours out on me."

"That's because you *are* the source of my frustration," he gritted out between clenched jaws as he pulled into the drive.

"No, Caldwell. I'm not the source. But I've got a pretty good idea who is." She scrambled out of the pickup and slammed the door behind her when he killed the motor.

Past the point of rational thought, he flew out of the truck, snagged her arm and spun her around to face him. "What the hell is that supposed to mean?"

She met his eyes with defiance. "Do you *really* want an answer to that?"

She was something standing there under the black Wyoming sky and a full moon that cast her face in silvery shadows and made her eyes glitter. She was mad and she was cruising for a target for that anger. He felt like one big bull's-eye.

There was a dare in her eyes, propelled by the hurt that fueled it. He realized suddenly that he knew what she was referring to. The thought hit him like a sledge. She'd spent another day with Bax who had a bad habit of thinking he knew what was best for him. And she'd spent time tonight with Sharon Russell who'd made it her mission in life to pair him up with every available female between Jackson Hole and Cheyenne. Between the two of them, they'd probably given her an earful about his ex-wife and their war of a marriage.

And, no, he didn't want an answer. Not from her. Not about this. He closed his eyes, felt a raw and outraged need to protect that small part of himself that Elise hadn't managed to destroy. He didn't want to know if this woman who incited feelings he'd sworn he'd never again submit to, could have any answers that he needed.

He didn't want to care about her, either. Yet, as they faced off in the moonlight, all he seemed able to care about was silencing that soft, sassy mouth with his, hauling her off to bed and making love to her until she was too exhausted to ask questions or give him grief.

Only, he knew that if he did that, his grief would just be beginning.

"No," he said finally. Releasing her, he stepped back, distancing himself both physically and emotionally. "I don't want an answer. What I want is to get some sleep."

She was still standing there, a small, defiant shadow bathed in moon glow and battling tears when he walked away.

It was a good half hour later before he heard the back door open, then close. Another before the door to her bedroom did the same.

But it was hours—long ones—before his mind let go of the picture she'd made. He'd never expected tears from her. From the way she'd stood there convulsively swallowing them back, he figured she hadn't, either. But what really blindsided him was the battle he was waging to keep from going to her. From holding her in his arms and telling her he was sorry that he was a bastard. Sorrier still that she was wasting her tears on the likes of him.

Once, a long time ago, he'd had something to offer a woman like her. Once, a long time ago, he'd had a heart worth mending. He'd even had a reason to want more out of life than to ride through it in silence and solitude.

"Editorial. Wells speaking."

"Hey, Mom, how's it going?"

"Kelsey?" Over the line, Kelsey heard Ed's feet hit the floor. "Is that you?"

"No, Einstein. It's Mother Goose."

"Why in blazes didn't you check in yesterday?"

She frowned at the phone. "I didn't know I was on such a short leash."

"If your father thought a leash would work, don't think he wouldn't have you on one."

She wrapped the phone cord around her finger and paced restlessly to the picture window. "Yeah, well, so what else is new? What's he on the rampage about this time?"

"Your whereabouts for one thing. Your choice of assignments for another."

She felt an unexpected disappointment swamp her. "You told him what I was doing?"

"Did Deep Throat leak the dirt on Watergate? Hell, yes, I told him! In case you forgot, he *is* the boss." His voice softened then. "In case you forgot something else—I'm also your friend, Kels. I didn't tell him everything. But I did have to confess that you're working on an angle about the leased land story that, if it pans out, could have far-reaching ramifications. Otherwise, he was going to make me call you in from the field."

She felt too much relief. She wasn't sure why. She just knew that other than Beth Langdon, who she could count on to keep this to herself, she didn't want anyone else aware of her speculations about the link between Caldwell and Montgomery. Not yet.

"Thanks, Ed. I owe you."

"You're right. You do. Tell me something—why is it you don't want to confide in the old man about this?"

"I have my reasons," she said softly, telling herself it was because she wanted to make sure she got the chance to break the exclusive herself. Convincing herself it had nothing to do with her renegade feelings for Caldwell and an escalating desire to protect him from the media mania her exposé on Montgomery could bring.

"So, how's it going?" Ed asked, sounding leery of her extended silence. "You getting what you need?"

Hardly, she thought dismally. What she needed was to get a certain cowboy out of her head and concentrate on her story. What she needed was to corral her emotions and toughen up. Sharon was wrong. Caldwell wasn't even the littlest bit interested in her. He'd proven that last night when he'd thrown away a perfect opportunity to own up to the possibility.

She forced herself to perk up. "It's coming together," she lied. "With a little luck, I should have things wrapped up in a couple of days," she added after a long silence.

"Well, that's good, because you've got another little problem."

She thought, regrouped, then frowned. "Not the Weasel?"

"The one and only."

Willis "the Weasel" Herkner was a perpetual pain in her heinie. A slimy little lowlife who claimed the title of "reporter" for a trash-and-flash supermarket tabloid called the *American Investigator,* Herkner inevitably showed up on the scene when she least wanted him around.

She pictured the Weasel's chinless, ferret face, slicked-back thinning blond hair and his short, tight plaid pants. It wasn't just his lounge-lizard looks that repulsed her. It was his underhanded methods and his nonexistent integrity.

"What's he up to?" she asked, fighting a wave of revulsion.

"I think the man has a crush on you, darlin'."

She groaned. "The next sound you hear is me gagging."

Ed chuckled. "The truth is, he was quizzing me about where you were and if what you were doing had anything to do with Montgomery."

She gripped the phone tighter as her heart slammed against her chest. "You're joking."

"Not this time."

"How could he have found out about this?"

"Settle down, kiddo. We don't know that he knows anything. I didn't tell you about it to rile you—just wanted you to be prepared if he was lying in wait for you when you got back.''

She forced a calming breath. ''You're right. Montgomery's the hottest item in the news these days. It would make sense that Herkner'd assume I might be covering some aspect of his campaign. He couldn't possibly know about my suspicions. No one could. Other than Beth—and I can bank on her silence until she hears from me.''

And no one else would, she told herself after she'd reassured Ed that all was well and hung up. No one would know unless she chose to tell them.

Once, that knowledge would have been a real power trip. Now it seemed like a burden. If she proved this story and broke it, it had the potential to ruin several lives. What had started out as a campaign to expose Montgomery as a fraud, because the people of America deserved to know the truth, now felt like sensationalism. Thinking about the Weasel and his slimy, exploitive ''journalism'' made her face, head-on, the implication that she might not be much better than he was. No longer could she dismiss the knowledge that whoever got hurt along the way was inconsequential as long as Montgomery got what he deserved.

She walked over to the window, stared through the glass and thought about Caldwell. What did he deserve in all this? Regardless of whether he was rude and remote and stubborn, did he deserve to have his paternity exposed and his life turned into a circus? Did his mother deserve an old and possibly painful wound to be reopened?

Guilt ate at her as she crossed her arms under her breasts and stared at the mountains. The steep, definitive lines cut earth from sky with bold, decisive strokes. Life used to be that clear-cut for her. The questions had been easy. The answers hadn't been so obscure. Not like now. Not since

Caldwell rode in, then out of her life that day on the top of the mountain.

"What about you, hotshot? What do you deserve from all this?" she asked herself dismally. She'd come here, convinced she deserved no less than the recognition and the notoriety an exclusive like this could bring. She'd come here bursting with righteous conviction.

Only, she didn't feel so righteous anymore. And she wasn't sure notoriety was enough. Caldwell had reduced her to tears last night. *Tears.* She'd never cried over a man. She'd never thought any man was worth it.

But Lucas Caldwell was different. And she'd begun to wonder if she deserved a chance to find out if her feelings for him were more than just a damnable combination of anger and lust. It didn't appear that she was going to be able to shake them. Not when she'd begun to eat and sleep and dream about the man.

Something this strong surely deserved a second look. And maybe—just maybe—she deserved the opportunity to at least confront the possibility that that cynical cowboy who'd ridden out on her *again* before sunrise felt something more for her, too.

She'd never met a man like Caldwell. Had never been intrigued to the point of wanting to look for more, or attracted to the point of losing sleep. She deserved to know if he was the exception worth exploring. And as she stood there, inspired by the mountains, driven by a frightening blend of need and desire, she finally came to the conclusion that she'd be the one dodging confrontation if she didn't face him with the possibilities.

She'd never know if he could care about her the way she'd finally admitted she cared about him if she didn't go after him. He sure as the world wasn't going to make any moves her way. Running the opposite direction was more his approach.

With a deliberateness born of a sudden and stubborn certainty, she headed for the kitchen and snagged her hat from the peg. Yeah. She deserved to know. And by God, whether Caldwell wanted to admit it or not, so did he.

Seven

"**R**un out on you again, did he, missy?"

When she spotted Bax in the dark shadows of the horse barn, she grinned and tucked her hands into the hip pockets of her jeans. "Lucky for me, I've got thick skin, huh?"

Bax chuckled. "I reckon it is."

"Well, what say you just reckon which direction he headed out this time and take me to him?"

Bax scrunched up one side of his face and scratched his stubbled jaw. "Well, now, it ain't gonna be quite that easy. Where he went today, you can only get to on horseback."

"Oh." That stopped her for a minute. But only a short one. She and Bax had four-wheeled it around the foothills of the Triple C on the two days they'd spent together. She'd figured they could head out the same way today in search of the elusive Mr. Caldwell.

"Oh, well," she said, confident that she was in too deep to back away now. "When in Wyoming. There's got to be something in this barn that won't take too much exception to having me on its back."

Bax grinned. "I figure Hester'll do just fine."

Every little girl, at one time or another, had romanticized about racing across a wild Western landscape, the wind in her hair, her horse fleet and sleekly muscled beneath her. Kelsey was no exception. She'd dreamed those sweet dreams. Many times. Hester, however, was not the stuff sweet dreams were made of. Hester was a bad dream. The kind that woke you in the night and sent you running to your mother.

A nightmare nag the likes of which she'd never seen, the aging sorrel quarter horse was a Roman-nosed, bald-faced, glass-eyed, broom tail who was as broad as she was tall. In addition to her stellar looks, she rode about as smooth as a garbage truck with shot shocks, and had a disposition as sour as spoiled milk. And if her looks and her attitude and her bone-rattling gait weren't enough to discourage any slim possibility of endearment, there was something else not to like about Hester. Hester bit.

"Just keep your toes up and an eye out," Bax advised as they'd headed out. "When she lays back her ears and rolls her eyes, that's a sure sign she's about to whip her head around and take a chomp. Just give the rein a stiff jerk and she'll come to tow."

After a few miles of fending off several of Hester's "love nips," Kelsey was past the point of worrying about the mare's bad habits. She was more concerned about staying on her back as they lumbered along a rocky trail that led to the high country. They'd been in the saddle since early morning and her tender bottom and unaccustomed muscles had begun to scream obscenities at her midway up the mountain slope.

Bax twisted in his saddle to check on her. "You doin' okay back there, missy?"

"Fine," she responded brightly, not wanting to let him see how soft she was or admit to any discomfort—discomfort, hell. She was in pain and she hated herself for the weakness. "Are we almost there?"

Bax just chuckled and headed on up the trail. She gritted her teeth and narrowly avoided losing the toe of her boot to another one of Hester's sneak attacks.

By noon, the sun was warm and bright, the sky a vibrant blue. While skifts of snow and the occasional deeper drift still patched the rock- and moss-covered mountain slopes, the grass was greening up and spring flowers were making their nodding debut. As she and Bax shared a hastily thrown together lunch Naomi had packed, she couldn't help but compare Wyoming favorably to the smog-drenched skies of L.A. She'd always been a city girl. A product of her environment. After these few days here in the shadow of the Big Horns, however, she wasn't sure she'd be able to readapt to the crowds and the noise and the lack of wide-open spaces. She wasn't even sure if she wanted to.

Unfortunately, the choice wasn't hers to make. The choice would be up to Caldwell. At least it would be if she held on to her nerve and accomplished what she'd set out to do on her jaunt up the mountain. She'd done more foolish things in her life but by two in the afternoon, she couldn't remember when.

When Bax finally pulled up, she figured her hour of reckoning was near. She coaxed Hester up beside him.

"Yonder," he said, nodding in the direction of a not-so-distant knoll. "That'd be him. He's been scouting strays, getting ready for the big drive up to the summer range. Looks like he's taking a little break."

Kelsey shaded her eyes with her hand. Following Bax's gaze, she first spotted Caldwell's big bay gelding, then the man himself standing with his back to them, about three city blocks from where they stood.

"You want I should take you all the way over there?"

"No," she said, gathering her courage as she slowly dismounted. "I'll walk from here. You take Hester back with you."

Grimacing in pain, fearing she was destined to spend the rest of her life wondering if there'd be room for a truck to drive between her bow legs, she handed Hester's reins to Bax.

Bax frowned. "You sure that's such a good idea?"

"If he shows up back at the ranch tonight without me, you'll know it wasn't." She pinched out a smile. "Just keep an eye out for me, okay?"

"Whatever you say," Bax returned with a wiry grin. "Well, what are you waiting for?" he prompted when she stood rooted to the spot, frowning at Caldwell's distant, ridged figure. "Just mosey on over there."

"I would," she grumbled with a pained wince and braced her hand on her lower back, "but I think maybe my mosey might be broken."

"Work it out, girl," Bax advised with a chuckle as he reined his mare and Hester around and headed back down the slope. "Work it out."

Bax was right. By the time she'd hiked to within twenty feet of where Caldwell stood, the worst of the pain had subsided to a dull ache. When he turned and spotted her, though, pain was the last thing she figured she had to worry about. Dead people didn't feel any pain, and the look on his face clearly suggested he wanted to strangle her.

Anticipation twisted sharply with apprehension as he glared at her, a silent, stoic figure backlit by sunshine and mountain peaks. He was dressed in soft, faded chambray and work-worn denim. His long legs were covered in supple leather chaps that cupped and framed his masculinity and quickened her heartbeat.

Bold with determination, wishing she hadn't worn the red shirt that made her such a bright target for his anger, she took another halting step toward him. He didn't move. He was as unyielding as the wind, as distant as the scattered herd speckling the greening valley behind him. And she was hopelessly in love.

It was frightening to finally admit the full-blown truth. Especially now. Now that she'd come to him. She felt a vulnerability so strong, it weakened her. Along with it, though, came a conviction so defined, it replenished that strength.

Love at first sight. The cliché was as old as dirt. Until she'd set eyes on Caldwell, she'd always figured its probability quotient was equivalent to a balanced national budget. And for a woman who'd rarely found a man worthy of her admiration, let alone her love, the concept should have been more difficult to embrace. Yet there it was. The only explanation. And as she watched him watch her, it was the only one that mattered.

She loved him and she was determined to let him know. She was also determined to believe that he wanted to care about her, too. The memory of the woman who'd shared that frilly feminine bedroom, however, was going to make it difficult. His past pain had perpetuated the distrust in his eyes and added to the lone-wolf aloofness he'd mastered. His bald accusation that Kelsey had intended to seduce him because she wanted something else from him hadn't come from a carefully nurtured suspicion of women in general. It was one woman in particular who was responsible.

It had taken a while for her to see past his cold eyes and hurtful accusations and put it all together. Now she understood. He hadn't just been burned. The part of him that had loved and shared and trusted had been charred beyond recognition. He wasn't about to reach into the fire again. Not without good reason.

Kelsey intended to give him that reason even though admittedly, to date, she'd only given him reason to be wary. And while it had been the story that had originally brought her to him, the story had been the farthest thing from her mind since he'd kissed her.

The fact that she'd just ridden across heaven and earth to find him was proof. She hadn't risked Hester's wrath and suffered a bruised bottom just to watch him stand there and stare at her with murder in his eyes. She wanted him to know how she felt. She wanted him to know it now before she lost her nerve.

"Aren't you going to say something?" she asked, hearing a quaver in her voice that betrayed a niggling uncertainty.

His expression didn't alter. Neither did his attitude. He watched her from that loose-hipped cowboy stance, one hand on his hip, his hat tucked low on his brow. Unapproachable. Unbending.

"What would you like me to say?"

"Nice day?" she offered with a game smile and a lift of her shoulders as her words drifted on the wind to reach him.

"For a ride," he added, stern-faced. "If you hurry, you can still catch one." He glanced pointedly over her shoulder to where Bax and Hester would be disappearing over the ridge about now. "Otherwise it's going to be a long walk back to the ranch. I wouldn't advise it in those boots."

"Tell me something, Caldwell," she said, propping her fists belligerently on her hips. "Do you practice being surly, or is it a gift?"

He gave her a hard stare. "I've got work to do."

In a blatant gesture of dismissal, he turned his back to her and bent to gather his gelding's reins where they trailed the placidly grazing horse across the grassy slope.

"Well, now, there's a surprise. You're taking off on me again. How original. You know, you really ought to change your act. You've done that one to death."

The slow, tense stiffening of his broad shoulders told her she'd hit a nerve. She also sensed the exact moment when he decided he was going to ignore her jab and ride away anyway.

"Coward," she accused, reckless in her conviction that it was time to make him face his feelings. "If you think I rode all the way up here just to watch you make another great escape, you've got another think coming, cowboy."

When he didn't turn around to face her, she didn't think past the fact that he was really leaving. She just reacted.

Reaching into a snow drift shadowed from the warm May sun by a boulder, she packed a baseball-size bullet and fired it as hard as she could.

Hard enough that the force sent her hat tumbling to the ground behind her. Hard enough that it hit him smack between his shoulder blades, impacting with a satisfying splat that spooked the gelding and sent him skittering.

Caldwell wasn't the skittering kind. He rounded on her with murder in his eyes.

Well, she'd been looking for a reaction. She got it. In spades. His dark eyes were narrowed and hot. His mouth was fixed in a grim, hard line. And she'd be willing to stake a winning lottery ticket that he'd changed his mind about leaving.

Self-preservation waged a stout battle with pride. Pride won. It usually did, which is why she always ended up in trouble. And trouble was something she was definitely in. He'd already taken one long stalking stride toward her before she managed to pack another missile. She hauled back and hurled it with a force her pumping adrenaline made lethal.

Bull's-eye. The snowball hit his hat and sent it sailing. A look somewhere between stark disbelief and black rage darkened his face. When he not only didn't stop to retrieve his hat but quickened his strides and zeroed in on her, self-preservation instincts finally kicked into overdrive.

"Now, Caldwell... don't do something you'll be sorry for," she cautioned him, realizing she might have pushed him a tad too far. The granite set of his mouth and the intent in his eyes warned her not to wait around to find out.

She whirled around and ran for her life—and was reminded how right he was. Her boots weren't made for walking. And running—well, running wasn't even a remote possibility. Not on this rocky terrain.

She hadn't gotten ten feet before he'd caught up to her, snagged her arm and spun her around to face him.

"If you came up here looking for trouble, Gates, you're about to get it."

"I came up here looking for some straight talk, *Caldwell,*" she shot back, finding her backbone again and refusing to cringe under his angry glare and his punishing grip on her arm. "Any prayer I'll get some of that, too?"

He went very still. "You tell me. You're the one who's been pussyfooting around the truth of why you showed up at my door."

He had a point there. One that had to be dealt with. She drew a deep breath. "Okay, how's this for the truth? You're right. I came here for a story. But guess what? I ended up falling in love. Yeah," she added, feeling as stunned as he looked that she'd blurted it out. "I agree. It's a real kick in the pants. And if it's any consolation, I'm not sure I like it much better than you do. But there it is anyway. A done deal. It doesn't make any sense, and I'm not fool enough to think you feel the same way but it hasn't seemed to make any difference."

Heart pounding, she stared him down, feeling more vulnerable and exposed than she ever had in her life. "*Now* what have you got to say?"

His expression grappled with denial and disbelief as he gripped her by both arms and dragged her nose to nose with him.

"I say you're a damn fool."

She blinked hard and swallowed the last of her pride. "Yeah, well, here's a news flash. There's one born every minute. Just my luck, I opted to be born all over again."

After a long, protracted look, he closed his eyes, drew a frustrated breath and swore.

She hung her head, damning herself for her reckless announcement of love... and for letting the hurt that he didn't return it creep in. Why hadn't she kept her big mouth shut? Talk about sticking a hand in the fire. Talk about feeling the burn. His hard eyes and angry scowl were as honest as it got.

Was this what they called poetic justice? She'd finally found a man worth loving and the odds of him loving her back were about as good as the chances of her developing some common sense. Slim and none.

She pinched back angry tears, wishing the rocky slope beneath her would open up, swallow her whole and get her the heck away from his glacial glare and painful grip.

The grip in question relaxed slowly, then with a subtle shift of muscle and sinew, became a hesitant, almost comforting caress. With puzzled hesitation, she raised her head and met his eyes.

What she saw there gave her pause. And, if she could believe it, hope. She blinked and looked again. But it was still there. A softness, an innate kindness. Even a gentle affection.

"You're really something, you know that?" he said with a gruff edge to his voice that could be either admiration, amusement, fatigue or all three.

She chose to believe it was all three—and maybe something more. Something like a caring that he was fighting to let himself feel. To think as much made it hurt less. To think as much implied there might be something to pin that thin wisp of hope on.

"Yeah," she managed with a conviction fueled by that hope, "Yeah. I know it. The question is, you hard-headed, jack-mule stubborn cowboy, do you?"

He shook his head, the barest hint of a regretful smile tugging at the corner of his mouth. "Tying up with me would give you nothing but grief. It's not even anything personal. I'm just not capable of returning your feelings. Don't try to fool yourself into thinking I can."

His words warned her off, yet his eyes asked her to stay. Like the eyes of a wolf, alone not by choice but by necessity, they caressed her face with a heat and hunger that gave her the courage to go on.

"Oh, it's personal all right," she whispered breathlessly. "Real personal. And I'm willing to take my chances.

I'm very adaptable. Over the years, I've become a master at settling for what I can get."

He searched her face long and hard. "You don't have any idea what you're asking."

"I know exactly what I'm asking." Her voice had softened with a rusty plea, an aching admission of her own need, banking on his to be her ally. "Please...don't make me ask again."

But she could see then that the time for asking was past. The time for reacting had begun.

His voice, gravelly and coarse, was completely at odds with the gentle brush of his lips as he lowered his mouth to her forehead. "Don't say I didn't warn you."

She swayed toward the whisper of contact. "I consider myself warned."

He sobered abruptly, gave her a hard shake and forced her to look him in the eye. "Do you? Do you *really* know it for a fact? I don't have anything to offer you. Nothing past today. Nothing more than now. Don't make the mistake of thinking you can change that. You can't. I've got nothing else in me to give."

It hurt. But she'd expected it to. Sure, she'd wanted more but she wasn't about to let him know that. Not yet. He was already offering more than she'd expected. She hadn't deluded herself into believing she could knock down a decade worth of walls in a day.

But she had every intention of making a liar out of him. In time, she would make him see he was safe with her. That he could take a chance and love again.

A journey of a thousand miles begins with one step. She'd made that first step. And while it had been a reluctant one, so had he. He'd warned her. He'd given her every opportunity to get out while the getting was good. He'd never admit it but it showed that he cared. If he didn't, he would have taken what she was offering without a qualm of guilt or benefit of warning.

"Caldwell," she whispered, freeing her arms from his grip and looping them around his neck. "For a man of few words, you picked a heck of a time to decide to get talkative. I know what I'm getting into, okay? You've done your duty. So stop with the warnings. And get on with what we both want. Today. Just today. Believe me when I tell you I'm not asking for more."

With a boldness she didn't want time to talk herself out of and an unimpeachable sense of rightness to lead the way, she stretched to her tiptoes and touched her mouth to his.

She felt the shudder rip through his big body. Sensed his reluctance, his hard-fought surrender. And felt, for the first time in her life, the strength of her power as a woman. A woman intent on making love to her man.

His body was hard and hot against hers. His lips were full and mobile and achingly soft. He tasted of sun and seduction and sweet, sweet need as he parted them beneath her touch and let her have her way.

She rimmed his mouth with the tip of her tongue. He groaned and closed his eyes, his breath catching as she scattered a string of light, nipping kisses across his jaw, then returned to his mouth again with a languor born of confidence.

A warm, delicious melting started at the point where her lips met his to cue them both that the fighting was finally over and the loving had officially begun.

His ragged breath relayed both a grudging defeat and a stunning desire as he gathered her against him. He opened his mouth wide, embracing her kiss with an urgency that was both searching and shocking. Both greedy and giving. Carnally explicit with the honesty of his need.

And she couldn't help but court the hope. On this sun-drenched mountain slope, with the sweet May breeze rustling the grass and playing with her hair, everything seemed right with her world. She let herself believe in a future he fervently denied and feast on sensations that swirled and spiraled and finally swept her away.

She murmured his name when he backed her up against the cool north side of a boulder and molded the searing heat of his body against hers. She whispered a plea when he moved against her, ridged and lean, straining and strong, nudging her with his strength and arousal. And she answered his deep-throated moan with a bold thrust of her hips, rising on her tiptoes to meet his insistent pressure.

Tangling one hand in his hair, she indulged in its thick, silken texture, splaying her other hand across the sun-warmed muscle of his back. He smelled like mountain wind and supple leather. His mouth tasted like temptation itself, drugging her with desire, seducing her body and soul. Responses laced with a richness she'd never dreamed of compelled her to lose herself in his heat and satisfy this yearning she'd never before known. Until him.

And all the while, this hard, unfeeling cowboy introduced her to a wealth of feelings that made her ache with both humility and need.

He didn't want to care about her, but he did. Every tongue stroke, every whisper of his big hands on her body convinced her of that. It was that special, tender care that combined with the beauty of the mountain, and the magic of the moment and prompted her whispered plea. "Make love to me."

Make love to me. Her seeking, breathy request shimmered through his blood like a riptide. It dragged him down, sucked him in, pulled him deep. Into her scent. Into her heat. Into a bronc-wild ride of turbulent passion and reckless desire.

Make love to me. He clung to his conviction that love had nothing to do with what he was feeling for her. Even if it did, he no longer cared about the risk. All he cared about was giving her what she wanted. And taking what had become his greatest need.

Her mouth was an offering of pleasure. The supple heat of her body a promise of the same. At the touch of his tongue, she came alive for him, a breathless combination of silk and honey and flame. Beneath his hands, hands that could enclose her small waist without effort and fit the saucy curves of her bottom into their palms, she moved with a restless yearning.

Holding her reminded him just how delicate she really was. How hot. How willing. How totally and honestly she responded to him. He wrapped her tighter against him, leaning her back against the boulder until pleasure blended sweetly with pain. She made him forget things. Simple things like common sense and persistent pain. His injured arm and hand reminded him with a vengeance that there were better places to make love to a woman. Her soft whimper did the same.

She deserved better. Any woman did. Better than him. Certainly better than a bruised backside. It was too late to save her from him now, but he could do something about the bruises. To do that, he'd have to slow things down.

Easing away from her, he threaded his hands through her hair to settle her. Problem was the lady didn't want to be settled.

She knotted her hands around his neck and dragged him back to her mouth, delving inside with deep, ravenous tongue strokes and wild, wicked abandon. And God help him, if she didn't quit rocking against his hips with such churning, burning invitation, he'd end up taking her against this cursed boulder after all.

"Kelsey," he whispered, cupping her face in his hands and forcing her to look at him. Her languid green eyes finally came into focus. "Kelsey...this is happening too fast. I don't want to hurt you."

"Hurt me?" she repeated in a voice that sounded detached and drained of comprehension as she sought his mouth again in another dangerous kiss. With a mind-bending little quiver, she pulled away, tugging his bottom lip between her teeth before nipping him lightly. "I already hurt," she whimpered and guided his hand to her breast. "Here. Make it go away."

Her lush fullness filled his palm. Her sigh of pure, wanton pleasure filled his chest with an ache that rivaled the one in his groin. With a groan of hard-fought control, he set her firmly away when she would have come back for another kiss.

She didn't care much for his tactics and let him know with a frustrated groan. She was no more frustrated than he. But he was a man who placed a high value on responsibilities. A randy sixteen-year-old could be forgiven for losing his head. A grown man couldn't—no matter how gut-tightening or pulse-elevating the reason.

He sucked in a ragged breath. "We need to slow this down. Kelsey, I don't have any protection."

"Protection?" She raked a silken fall of hair from her eyes, then moistened her kiss-swollen lips. When his meaning hit home, a relieved look washed over her face. "Caldwell...I'm not going to get pregnant."

Myriad emotions played through his head—and evidently across his face. Whatever she saw there, she decided she didn't like it. Nor did she like the silence she was hearing.

"Oh," she said, sounding enlightened with a wisdom that came from hurt. "Oh, I get it. The protection isn't for me, is it? It's for you." She shoved him hard in the chest. She wasn't any stronger than a kitten but she had surprise on her side. He stumbled backward as if he'd been broadsided by a Brahman, instead of by a woman who'd suddenly developed a disposition like one.

Showing him her back, she hugged her hands around her waist. When she spoke, he could hear the effort it was taking to sound strong and composed.

"An unplanned pregnancy is the last thing I need in my life, Caldwell. I wouldn't do that to myself—or to you. And for the record, cowboy, if you're worried about disease, I don't sleep around." She glanced over her shoulder at him, the paleness of her face revealing how achingly vulnerable she was. And how much he'd hurt her. "You're safe with me. I can't hurt you. I wouldn't if I could. But, hey, believing that would require a major leap of faith, wouldn't it? I guess it's a little too much to ask to stretch things that far between us."

His head was starting to ache more prominently than other critical parts of his body. He was botching this. Badly. And if her ego as well as her self-esteem hadn't been at stake here, he might have let it lie. He sure as hell didn't need the aggravation making love to her would bring.

Like hell, he didn't. He was past trying to figure out the whys and the hows and the wrongs of it. He only wanted to make that look go away. The one that said, I'm hurting, I'm not as tough as I want you to think I am. The one that said, Don't you dare feel pity for me.

"You think you're pretty good at reading between the lines, don't you?"

Her chin came up but her arms wrapped tighter around her waist. "Yeah, well, I've had a lot of practice. Some rejections are simply more subtle than others. I'm usually a little quicker on the uptake.''

As he'd suspected from the beginning, the animosity she felt for her father was grounded in a motive less frivolous than rebellion. She showed a tough side for a reason—so no one could guess she was struggling with feelings of inadequacy.

"You are such a fraud," he said gently, touching a finger to her petal-soft cheek as he walked past her on the way to pick up his hat and hers.

"And you are such a jerk."

He didn't let her see his grin as he settled his hat on his head. The bay reluctantly raised his head from his grazing as Lucas gathered the reins.

"That's one thing you've got right," he said, leading Coop back to Kelsey's side. "I'm out of practice at this. I never was much good at it in the first place. I didn't mean to hurt your feelings. I didn't mean to hurt you."

He paused, staring at the reins gripped loosely in his hands before handing her her hat. Letting out a deep breath, he met her eyes. "I simply want to make love to you so badly, I can't think past the wanting."

Her eyes rounded with surprise and a pleasure held in check by disbelief.

"But it's my responsibility to think about it. There's a right way and a wrong way to do this, Kelsey. I want to do it right. Ride down the mountain with me." His heart melted at the gradual, prideful softening in her eyes. "When we get there, I'll show you how right it can be."

Eight

For all of her earlier bravado, she suddenly became shy with him. He'd have smiled if he was sure she wouldn't think he was laughing at her. Laughing at her right now would be dangerous—for her self-esteem, which he'd determined by now had taken quite a beating over the years, and for himself. She looked that far from hauling off and decking him if he so much as looked at her wrong.

"Kelsey..." His voice was a soft but steady command as he held out his hand. "Come with me."

He read the struggle behind those wide green eyes and marveled at the change in her. Shyness definitely became her. And her submission, as she made that halting step toward him, nearly blew him away.

He didn't give her a chance to dwell on what she'd thought was rejection—past, present or future. They'd deal with it when the time came. The time for them was now. And while he hadn't admitted it then, the time for denying it had passed the moment he'd first set eyes on her.

He reached for her, drawing her into his arms and into a kiss that tested his determination to wait until he got her back to his bed so he could love her the way she deserved to be loved.

When he raised his head, the questions in her eyes were the questions woman had asked man for all eternity. In the drift of his hands across her body, he gave her the answers she needed.

He stroked her cheek lovingly, giving in to a gentleness he'd forgotten he possessed and that felt achingly good to express. He told her with his touch how beautiful he found her, then showed her with his caress how that beauty stoked his need. And he convinced her with a tenderness that, before Kelsey, he hadn't thought he had in him.

"I'm not a kid anymore, Kelsey," he said, feeling an overwhelming need to set her at ease. "I haven't shown my bare backside to the sun since I was sixteen and skinny-dipping in a watering hole. I can't see myself doing it now... no matter how tempting it is to strip you bare and take you here and now."

A soft blush stained her cheeks.

Again he touched a hand there. "So we wait, okay? I want the assurance of your privacy when I make love to you." He brushed the hair out of her eyes with a gentle hand. "Now, please, mount up before I forget I'm forty and that Toby Wheeler is just over the next rise scouting strays and apt to ride up on us at any moment.

"But know this..." He tipped her face to his with a curled finger under her chin. "Before this day is over, I *am* going to make love to you." Her eyes betrayed her pleasure, then her shock when he added decisively, "Several times, I think. And if you keep looking at me that way, you can bank on it."

She seemed to forget her anger and let go of her hurt as they made their way slowly down the mountain. But he damn well couldn't forget her heat and hunger. And she wasn't about to let him.

The lady had a mission. To make him pay for his ineptness at bruising her tender sensibilities. To make him sweat for choosing to wait. To keep him granite hard and cursing the gods of perpetual torment for deciding not to make love to her when the moment had demanded it.

Instead, he had to endure the sweet torture of the long ride back to the ranch with her nestled in the saddle in front of him. He wasn't sure if it was innocence, instinct or invention that had her shifting her slim little backside just so—until she ended up pressing into and nudging against an arousal that threatened to burst the buttons on his fly.

He wasn't even sure if he was going insane or simply sinking deeper under her spell as he drew her back against him, removed her hat and lowered his mouth to her hair. Drowning in her fragrant, sunny heat beating against him, he guided Coop down the trail toward home and circled Kelsey's waist with one hand. The silk of her hair tickled and teased his cheek as she relaxed with a sigh, then turned her face to his for a lazy, drugging kiss.

As natural as breathing, his hand rose to claim the delicate arch of her throat, cupping her jaw, adjusting the fit of their mouths, increasing the intimacy of the kiss. His hand descended unerringly to her chest, then lower to cup and entice her breast to a ripe awakening.

She arched into his hand, her own hands gripping his leather-covered thighs where they rode in a sensual rhythm on either side of hers. Unbuttoning her blouse, he slipped his hand inside as he plunged his tongue deep into her mouth.

Silk and velvet. Against his mouth, against his palm. Her cushiony weight and yielding flesh filled his hand as he stroked her with tongue and fingertips to a liquid, budding arousal. When the tip of her breast pebbled against his fingers, he sucked in a harsh breath of sheer unadulterated lust.

She tore her mouth from his, biting her lower lip between her teeth with a throaty moan. "Caldwell," she whimpered, nuzzling her cheek in restless frustration into the hollow beneath his jaw. "I don't think I'm going to make it."

He muttered an oath and touched his lips to her hair to settle her. Then easing his hand from the warmth beneath her shirt, he reined in Coop.

"I'm too damn old for this," he muttered, drawing a deep breath. "There's got to be a better way."

Without waiting for her suggestion, he dismounted, readjusted his aching arousal to a less painful position and motioned for her to scoot back.

"We'll try it with me in front. Maybe that way I won't be so tempted."

"And how's that supposed to help me?" she asked with a shaky grin as she buttoned up, then did as he asked and made room.

"It's not," he said gruffly as he eased carefully into the saddle in front of her. "It's supposed to get us back to the ranch house without emasculating me."

It turned out to be another good idea that didn't work. The girl had busy hands. The girl had a way of driving him wild and a special talent for pressing those beguiling breasts of hers into the flat of his back and sending him over ten different edges in ten different ways. Some of them sweet, all of them sexy, not to mention painfully effective.

He couldn't convince her to leave him alone. His heart—as well as other parts of his body—really wasn't in it. Which is why three long, hot hours later, with the sunset nipping at their heels, he was as lathered up as his horse when they hit the valley at a fast lope.

Lucas sent Kelsey to the house, intending to make fast work of bedding down the horse, then making sure there weren't any problems in need of his attention. He had a need of his own that needed tending—an immediate one—and for once, it was going to take precedence. Just as soon as he dealt with Bax. The old cowhand had met him at the gate, then hung around Coop's stall, leaning against it with a casualness too staged to be real.

"Something on your mind, Bax?"

"Maybe."

"Be best if you just spit it out, don't you think?"

Bax cleared his throat, then hooked his thumbs in the low riding buckle of his belt. "Appears you two have come to an understanding," he said in a tone Lucas recognized as both judgmental and questioning.

Lucas grunted, figuring he knew where this was headed. He tossed a forkful of hay into the manger. Swinging the door to the pen shut, he waited the older man out. He didn't have to wait long.

"Appears to me you let yourself get in a little deep on this one, Lukey."

Lucas stopped, thumbed back his hat and hung his hands on his hips. "And it occurs to me that news ought to suit your purpose just fine," he said with a grim scowl.

"You've been pushing her on me since the day she set foot on Triple C ground."

Bax scratched his jaw and said with a glum scowl, "I reckon I have."

"Then what's the problem?"

Bax's faded eyes pinned him with a look. "It'd be a shame if she was to get hurt."

"Maybe you should have thought about that before you brought her to me today."

The old cowhand shifted his weight from one bandy leg to the other. "Maybe I shoulda. And maybe you shouldn't blame one woman for another woman's poison."

Lucas let out a deep breath. Bax was wrong. This wasn't about Elise. About getting even, or paying back. At least he told himself it wasn't. It was bad enough he'd let his ex-wife turn him into a loner who justified his aversion to any lasting relationship with distrust. He prayed to God he hadn't let her also make him into a man who leveled justice on the closest outlet for his anger.

"I don't want to hurt her, Bax," he said, meaning it.

The old man's face relaxed, his eyes relaying a guarded satisfaction. "Then see to it that you don't."

"She's a big girl. And she knows the rules. So if this doesn't come down the way you think it should, don't pin all the blame on me."

With a long, meaningful look, he turned and left Bax standing in the shadows. With long purposeful strides, he headed for the house, telling himself everything he'd just told Bax was true.

Kelsey wasn't taking any chances. That's why she'd hedged her bets on the ride back to the ranch. At great cost to both of them. Once she'd gotten a commitment from

Caldwell, she'd wanted to keep their mutual goal firmly embedded in his mind.

Making love. Making peace. Making inroads in that armored guard of his that had sent him off in the opposite direction for the last time—she hoped.

He'd told her he'd be no more than an hour. That he had things he had to take care of first.

"Life as he knows it does not cease to exist just because he'd decided to make love to you," she reminded herself as she eased out of the tub and reached for a towel. "Even though life as you know it has."

She wiped the steam from the mirror and checked her reflection. She looked the same. No visible changes. Nothing that would indicate that a woman whose sexual adventures to date could fit on the head of a pin with room left over for an elephant, had turned unexpectedly into a vamp. A quick, clumsy, curiosity tumble in the back seat of a car with another eighteen-year-old virgin, and a disappointing short-term relationship with a man she'd thought she loved, but had never pleased either in bed or out of, was the sum total of her experience. Nothing to pin all this hope on. Certainly not enough to deliver on the promises her busy hands and outrageous performance had implied.

"This falls under the 'all's fair in love and war' department," she assured herself staunchly. "Women have been seducing men since creation to get what they want.

"Besides, it's the motive, not the method that matters here," she added as she drenched herself in jasmine, sandalwood and ylang-ylang, a hurriedly blended mix of fragrant essential oils all noted, among other things, for their aphrodisiac qualities. Then she prayed that what she lacked in experience would come naturally.

In her mind, she continued to justify the seduction. After all, she didn't want anything from the man. She wanted something *for* him. To share something good and giving, and maybe, just maybe, open him up to the idea that she wasn't the worst thing in the world that could happen to him. If anything was supposed to happen past that point, it would. And she'd deal with it, whatever it was, when it did.

Until then, she didn't plan on playing fair. She planned on playing to win. Taking a quick look around the bathroom, she made sure everything was set in here. Satisfied, she lit the candles and dropped the bottle with the note into the bathwater. Then, wrapping one of his huge, thirsty bath towels around her, and raiding his medicine cabinet of a handful of condoms, she headed for her bedroom.

Her room was at the end of the hall. She set the stage in there, then left her door open a crack so she could hear, even if she couldn't see his movements when ten minutes later, the back door opened. Soft, slow boot steps sounded down the hallway. Heavy, fast heartbeats echoed inside her chest. She sat tensely on the edge of the bed, seeing him in her mind's eye as he paused by the bathroom door, then turned and went into his bedroom.

The house was sunset quiet. She wished her thoughts were as tranquil. She held her breath, listening to the pounding of her blood through her ears and the dull thud of his boots falling where he'd tossed them. To the subtle sounds of first his shirt and then his jeans hitting the floor by the boots.

The bathroom door opened but didn't close. Her heart tripped again as she imagined his surprise, and she hoped his pleasure, when he discovered what she'd done. Imagined the soft light and flickering dance of the candle glow playing off the deep tan of his skin. Imagined him inhaling deeply of the sensual scent permeating the small room, and imagined, with a smile this time, his thoughts when he spotted the bottle with her message inside, floating in the bathwater.

By the time the water had gurgled from the tub and he'd finished his shower, anticipation had reduced her to a fidgety mass of blushing flesh and second guesses. The sun had made its gradual descent behind the mountain range, leaving the only light in the bedroom the one cast by the flames of the four candles she'd placed beside the four condoms on the nightstands by the bed.

The bed. It seemed so big suddenly as she gave in to the niggling thought that she just might be spending another night in it alone. Maybe he'd had too much time to cool off. And maybe she'd had enough time to come to her senses. Two big maybes pitted against one huge for sure. For sure, she would not lower herself to go after him again. It was now-or-never time. He only had to run as far as his own room this go-round and it would be far enough.

She closed her eyes and swallowed. When she opened them, her door was fully open, too—and so was the look in the eyes of the man leaning against the doorframe, taking in the candles, the condoms and her.

She could have cried with relief when she saw him standing there. She probably would have if she hadn't been so taken with the picture he made. Her gaze skimmed shyly over the long, lean length of his body, snagging momentarily on the towel knotted low at his hips and provocatively tented. She swallowed hard, entranced by the shadows that danced across damp skin still glistening from his shower, taken by the lush thickness of his hair, still wet and shining like burnished sable in the candle glow.

"You came." It was barely a whisper. Little more than a sigh. Two small words laced too liberally with relief. She hadn't intended for him to hear it.

But he must have. His eyes softened. So did her heart when he actually smiled. A first. A wonder. A joy that made her heart swell and her eyes mist.

"I had to. I had to find out the question," he said, holding up both the bottle she'd floated in the tub and the note she'd tucked inside. The note that read "The answer is yes."

Beneath the red silk of her nightshirt, her skin had taken on a new sensitivity. An enriched awareness of the touch of his hands, a shimmering anticipation of the wet silk of his mouth. She inched slowly toward the center of the bed and leaned back against the pillows.

"Pick a question," she suggested with a huskiness she hoped didn't reveal how nervous she was. "Any question. The answer will be yes if you want it to be."

With that invitation, she'd let herself be wide open to another rejection. But she needed to be sure. If he asked the right questions, she would be. The protection she'd found and displayed were her gesture of trust. Her way of saying she understood. He'd already lost one child to a woman. He wasn't willing to take the risk that it would happen again.

With his gaze locked on hers, he walked slowly to the bed and stood beside it. "Are you still sure this is what you want?"

"Yes." The answer came without hesitation. Without shame. "And yes, that was the right question."

He eased a hip onto the bed beside her, his gaze releasing hers to travel down her body in a slow, visual caress. He lingered overlong on the rise of her breasts beneath red silk, then strayed lazily to the spot where the hem of her nightshirt drifted to the top of her thighs. Her entire body tightened at the suggestion shimmering in his eyes as they lowered to the length of her bare legs before climbing leisurely back to her face.

She'd once thought those lone wolf eyes were unreadable. She'd been wrong. Everything he was feeling was relayed in them now. Everything she wanted to feel as a woman—beautiful, desirable, invincible—the look in his eyes made it all possible.

"Do you want me to touch you, Kelsey?"

She swallowed, aroused and moved by the ragged need in his request. "Yes," she whispered, then managed to say on a sigh she had no idea was brazenly seductive, "you're two for two, cowboy."

He smiled as his big hand reached for her, moving in a sure, possessive caress along her cheek before dropping to her shirt, then slipping open the covered buttons.

"Here?" he asked in a gruff whisper when he'd laid open the silk and covered her bare breast with his hand. "Like this?"

"Yes." More plea than acquiescence, she stirred beneath his hand, closing her eyes at the sweet, aching contact. "Oh, yes."

And then she lost track of the questions, lost count of his perfect score, as watching her face, he twisted at the hip and leaned over her. Planting his hands on either side of her shoulders, he braced his weight above her and dipped his head to her breast.

She cried out when he took her into his mouth, arching into his wet heat as his tongue played bold games against her nipple, his teeth nipping and tormenting with a pleasure so exquisite, it flirted with pain. A pain he soothed with gentle tongue strokes, then rekindled with a hungry suckling, telling of his need, demanding in his passion.

She became lost in sensation then. In the shift of weight and position. In the steely strength of his body stretched out next to hers. In the riotous rush of physical desire as he covered her mouth with his, delving inside with his tongue as his fingers found her woman's heat and explored with the same seductive, artful invasion.

Lucas had known that once he'd let this happen, there'd be no stopping it. That's why he'd fought it tooth and nail. What he hadn't known was the force with which it would take him. Or the fascination that would lead him to an unquenchable hunger to taste, and tease, and test his limits and her responses.

He'd thought he could keep this under control. He'd thought he could impose those limits. But limits weren't an issue. Boundaries weren't a factor. She was. The only issue. The overriding factor. Pleasing her. Loving her. Taking her where the trembling reply of her sleek, silken body told him she'd never been before.

He should have known. Somewhere, in that part of him that hadn't wanted to see her for what she really was—a pretender protecting her own damaged heart—he suspected he had known. Kelsey Gates, his sassy, brassy tormentor, who'd boldly raided his medicine cabinet, then brazenly displayed the protection he'd insisted on using, had managed to surprise him again.

For all her aggressive maneuvering to get him to this point, the lady was not experienced at love. Each straining, guileless response, each startled whimper of surprised pleasure, confirmed that knowledge. Her shivering sighs, her lush wet heat melting against his fingers was a rare gift he treasured and enjoyed and stretched to the farthest reaches of her untried passion.

He raised his head and searched her face. Her eyes were dazed with discovery, glazed with desire, as he stroked and stirred and brought her to the brink of release.

"Caldwell," she gasped, grasping his wrist in her small hand and stilling his circular motion.

"Shh. It's okay. Just go with it," he whispered, dropping a kiss to her temple. "It's good?"

"Yes," she managed to say, then closed her eyes again on a groan and arched into his palm. "Yes."

He hadn't meant to shock her. He'd only meant to pleasure her and indulge in a fantasy she'd created. But her breathy little sigh caught on a cry as he dipped his fingers deep inside her. And her eyes widened in stunned disbelief as he brought his hand to her breast and bathed its pebbled crown with the honeyed wetness coating his fingertips.

His groin ached at the sight of her pale plump flesh and the moisture glistening there, scented of her, and of sex, and a sweetness he couldn't resist. He lowered his mouth, drinking her in, sipping leisurely, licking lavishly, tasting her essence and taking her higher.

She tunneled her fingers through his hair, holding him close, begging him, "Please...please," with a restlessness that told him she didn't yet know what she was asking of him.

He planned to enlighten her. Just as soon as he'd tasted his fill...of her breasts, and her belly, and the moist heat hidden by downy soft curls that beckoned him lower. Just a taste. Just a deep, drugging drink that drove him wild with wanting and sent her soaring over the edge in a series of sweet wild cries.

A man had limits. He reached his when she dug her fists into the bedclothes and arched her hips into the pressure of his intimate invasion.

Sliding in one smooth, purposeful motion up her body, he reached for a condom and rolled it on. With a slow, deep glide, he entered her. And the fascination began again.

She was tight, velvet heat, surrounding, clenching, swallowing him alive and electrifying him with power. He filled her open mouth with his tongue, catching her heady moan with his breath, matching the sure, deep pumping of his hips as she rose to meet him.

"Caldwell," she whispered, again and again, her voice rich with the depth of her pleasure, ripe with the awakening of her desire, strained with the wonder of yet more discovery.

Power as potent as brandy, passion as heady as wine surged through his blood in an intoxicating rush of thick, molten heat. The inner walls of her body convulsed around him, draining him of control, driving him deeper, deeper, into the wonders of her body and the fire that was her soul.

She climaxed again in a series of panting, sultry cries that rocketed him to his own pulsing, grinding end. Driving them a full foot up the bed, he buried himself inside her with a blinding rush toward the sweetest release he'd ever known.

And above the rush of blood pounding through his ears and the ragged breaths that filled the silent aftermath of passion, her whispered "Yes" echoed in the darkness, a soft, awed affirmation of the love they'd just shared.

Like the calm in the wake of a storm, they lay sated and spent. A light sheen of perspiration gilded the soft curves of Kelsey's body. Lucas trailed his knuckles between her breasts, marveling at her softness, still shaken by the fierceness of her passion.

She turned her head to his on her pillow. Her eyes, liquid, jade pools, glittering by candlelight, misted over as she touched her palm to his jaw. He covered her hand in his and brought her fingertips to his mouth.

Her smile was as tentative as the night breeze rustling the curtains as she traced the outline of his lips with her fingertips. "Give a little answer, get a great big question."

He smiled at the smug languor in her voice.

"I like that almost as much," she added, propping up on an elbow to look down at him.

"You like what almost as much?"

"Your smile."

He rolled to his back, dragging her with him until she was sitting astride him. Her cheeks flamed, the color as vibrant as the silk of her hair when he positioned her intimately against his hips.

Lord, she was a beauty. Her lips were kiss swollen, her breasts quivering and peaked, gilded by a slice of moonlight slivering through the window.

"Since you like it so much," he whispered, feeling his need for her stir against her bottom, "here's your chance to see it again."

One corner of her mouth tipped up in a woman's smile of sheer, unadulterated power.

She leaned into his touch as he covered her breasts with his hands and kneaded softly. "I plan on taking lots of chances before this night is over."

"I suspected as much when I saw the candles and—"

"And these?" she suggested, as she leaned provocatively across him and reached for another condom.

Before settling her weight back on his, she caught his eye and blew out one of the four candles.

He glanced from her face to the remaining three, then back to her face again. "Why do I get the feeling that was your equivalent of putting a notch on a gun?"

Her smile was nothing short of wicked. "There you go with that cowboy mentality. It's just my way of—"

It was his turn to interrupt. "—Overestimating my stamina?" She only smiled and lovingly, if inexpertly, dealt with the protection.

"I'm willing," she said with a sultry, shimmery sigh as she settled herself with an exquisitely slow glide onto his heat, "to put your stamina to the test."

Embedded in her sleek, wet heat, he was willing to pass any test. Scale any mountain. Beat any odds as he gripped her slim hips in his hands and guided her to ride the sure, sensual rhythm he set. A rhythm that left doubt in the dust and raced the wind to the prize her sweet sexual healing promised.

Dawn rose to one guttering candle, one remaining condom and the primary light in the bedroom made by the woman lying next to him in bed.

His body felt drained. His chest felt achingly full as he watched her sleep, stroking a hand lingeringly across the pale satin of her bare hip. She stirred in her sleep, burrowing like a kitten into the sheets. Burrowing like a sure, steady fever into his blood, into his heart.

His hand stilled. Rolling to his back and away from her, he crossed his hands behind his head and stared at the ceiling. His heart wasn't supposed to be involved in this. His heart was supposed to be immune.

But she was more than he'd anticipated. More woman, more life, more to walk away from than a night he'd never forget.

What she lacked in sexual experience she made up for in enthusiasm. Bold in her discoveries, delighted with her power over him, she'd fulfilled his wildest fantasies with her lack of inhibitions and lusty, wild abandon. She'd managed to make him smile again, even laugh, a sound rusty from lack of use, as they ate a midnight meal in the middle of her bed. And later, much later, she'd made him moan again, too, with her exotic herbal oils, her smooth masterful hands, and the amazing manipulations of her eager, untutored mouth.

"Caldwell?"

He turned his head to see her peeking up at him from a drift of covers and a mop of beautifully mussed hair.

"What time is it?" she murmured with a sleepy sigh and slipped to his side, nestling trustingly against him as if she woke up with him every morning.

He told himself it was an involuntary reaction when he folded his arm around her, then covered the leg she'd slung across his thighs with his hand. Then, because it felt so good, he told himself it was time to put a little distance between them.

"Time to get up. At least it is for me. You sleep in."

He felt her yawn against his chest and fought the notion of how right it felt to hold her this way.

"Are you trying to run out on me again?" There was a soft smile in her accusation. A smile that intensified the ache in his chest and added to his misery.

"Running out's not the issue," he said, hoping the gruffness in his voice didn't relay just how big an issue it really was. He could get used to this. Too used to it. Kelsey was an indulgence he couldn't afford. "The work doesn't stop just because..."

His words trailed off when her sleep-warmed body squirmed suggestively against his and her small, seeking hand found him beneath the sheets and took him in a single stroke to rock-hard arousal.

"Because we just spent the most incredible night in this bed?" she suggested, raising on an elbow to press a slow, licking kiss to his nipple.

He swallowed back a groan. "Kelsey...I've got...work to do."

She raised her head, her hair tumbling into her eyes, her smile sultry and playful and bold. "And I'm just the woman you need to work on. It'd be a shame," she added, leaning across his body, provocatively and intentionally brushing her breasts against his chest as she reached toward the nightstand for the one remaining condom, "a real shame, if we were to let this go to waste."

He snatched it out of her hand and rolled her beneath him. Wanting to be angry, wanting to be anything but enchanted by the fire in her eyes and the wickedness of her smile, he growled, "Has anyone ever told you you're a terrible tease?"

"Am I...really?" she asked on a gasp, as lost in the wonder of her, he parted her thighs and sank deep.

He buried his face against her neck as defeat gave way to delirium. "The worst."

She hooked her ankles around his waist and hung on while he rocked into her with urgent, driving strokes. "I'm sorry."

"No, you're not," he murmured, threading his fingers through her hair as he gripped her face in both hands and captured her cry of release with his mouth. "And neither am I."

Another lie. He was sorry. Sorry he'd ever let it get this far. Sorry it could go no further. Sorry that she made him feel more of a man than he'd felt in his lifetime.

Most of all, he was sorry that he had no choice but to end it as soon as possible.

Nine

Kelsey wasn't sure, exactly, when she'd physically felt the emotional distance begin to grow between them. As she rode Hester, watching Caldwell's silent, brooding figure ahead of her on the trail, however, she suspected it was before he'd even risen from her bed this morning. Before he'd withdrawn from her body.

She'd been afraid it would happen. She'd hoped for more. More time with him. More chances to show him how good they could be together. Even more time to fool herself into thinking he wasn't going to end it.

But he was going to end it. He'd made that clear from the beginning. If he had his way, it would be a clean, swift break. If she had hers, there would be nothing clean or swift about it.

After a breakfast that was as awkward as it was silent, she'd swallowed her pride and followed him to the barn. When he'd suggested he had work to do that wouldn't interest her, she'd insisted he saddle up Hester for her and she'd ridden along anyway. Whatever excuse he'd manufactured, she was determined he wasn't going to ride away from her this morning. Not this golden, sun-drenched morning after the most beautiful night of her life.

She'd hate him for what he was doing—if she didn't love him so much. What a fool she was. What a twittering, dithering fool. He'd issued his warnings yesterday on the mountain. She'd told him she knew the perimeters. But last night in his arms, the boundaries had changed. She wanted more than just one night to get to know Lucas Caldwell for the man that he was, not the man he wanted people to see.

As Hester took another chomp at the toe of her boot, Kelsey automatically gave the rein a tug, then urged the stubborn mare into a trot. She drew up alongside Lucas as they topped a gently sloping ridge.

He reined his big bay to a stop. In silence, they shared the breathtaking view of the valley, one more thing she'd grown to love—and was going to lose. She looked out over the sweeping vista to the towering peaks to the west. Her own significance seemed vastly diminished in light of the total scheme of things. Her loneliness, however, took on greater magnitude as she remembered with bittersweet retrospection, the urgency in the way he'd last made love to her.

Made love. Made magic. Made history. At least for her. She'd never known it could be like that between a man and a woman. She'd never dreamed there could be so much pleasure—or such a sense of belonging, of being unconditionally loved for what she was, not what she was expected to be. In his arms, beneath his touch, she'd felt complete for the first time in her life.

And it hurt that he was determined to throw it away. No matter how cold and distant he was this morning, she knew it had meant something to him, too. There had been more than physical desire in his lovemaking. Much more than a sizzling rush of wild sexual heat. His hunger had spoken of a deeper longing. A poignant tenderness that had revealed the depth of his loneliness. An urgency that told of his struggle not to give in to his own needs but to tend with exquisite detail to hers. And in those unforgettable moments when their bodies had come together and she'd felt his honest strength envelop her, a yearning awakened in her to fulfill every one of the needs he denied as his own.

He wasn't about to let her do that. She glanced at him and drew a deep breath. Damn stubborn cowboy. Well, hell. She could be just as stubborn. And she wasn't going to make it easy for him to throw away the best thing that had ever happened to either one of them.

His loving had moved her too deeply. Left her drained and aching and renewed with a love that rocketed past any emotion she'd ever known. She was determined—for his own good as much as hers—to at least try to make him see how much he needed her. To make him acknowledge that he wasn't the cold, hard man his brooding silence suggested.

"You're awfully quiet," she began, hating the inane lameness of the opener but too tense to come up with something better.

"As you pointed out yesterday—I'm a man of few words."

It was cuttingly clear that he wanted it over. Too bad. Since there was no way it would be anything but painful for her, she had no intention of making it easy for him, either.

"A few more wouldn't hurt you." Even to her own ears, she sounded wounded and uncertain. Give me something here, her eyes pleaded. Something to pin some hope on and make a liar out of your indifference.

He folded his gloved hands across the pommel of his saddle and shifted his weight. The brim of his hat shaded the high morning sun and shadowed the hooded look in his eyes. "This conversation is beginning to reek of expectation, Kelsey," he said, as he stared straight ahead across the valley.

The stark warning in his statement stole her breath. "Wounded" no longer covered how she felt. "Bleeding and dying" did. The man had a knack for cutting to the quick. She stared at his lean, hard profile as anger nipped at the heels of her pain and stiffened her backbone ramrod straight.

"Expectation? Oh, well, God forbid I should expect anything from you other than the sight of you walking away." While she wasn't proud of her sniping reply, it was either rail at him or cry like a baby.

He hunched his shoulders and breathed deeply. With a weary shake of his head he reined Coop around and faced her. "Kelsey, I never set out to hurt you. And I never lied to you. I told you from the beginning this wasn't going anywhere."

Defiant, she lifted her chin and leveled a carefully thought out accusation. "Because of your failed marriage."

He didn't pretend to misunderstand. But it was only after a long, silent moment that he said, "Elise has nothing to do with this."

In an exploding rush of panic, she burst out with one of the fears she'd been fighting to deny. "If she doesn't have anything to do with this, then why is it that she's been gone for ten years and that bedroom is still waiting, untouched, for her to return?"

His mouth grew hard. "It's not waiting for her return. It's my reminder that I can't afford that kind of..." He hesitated, searching, then finally finding a word that satisfied him. "Investment of time and energy again."

"Ah." Her smile was bitter. "Investment. And I suppose that's how you see me—as a poor investment?"

"I see you as an ambitious young woman with bigger fish to fry. Hell, Kelsey, think about it. This isn't where you belong. Wyoming and I are just a stopover for you. A temporary diversion. You know it as well as I do."

"How dare you sit there and tell me what you are to me!"

He looked at her long and hard but refused to rise to the bait. "Let it go, Kelsey. We shared something good. But we both knew when we started that it wasn't forever. You said you understood that up front."

"I lied," she shot back without shame, then turned her face away so he couldn't see the tears that had suddenly crowded her eyes. "I don't want this to be over," she said in a voice stripped of pride, then raised her face to his again. "I want it to just be beginning."

His hard eyes softened. "It's no good, Kelsey. *I'm* no good. Not with relationships. Not when it counts."

"And you base that conclusion on the sum total of your experience with one woman?" She heard the desperation in her voice but couldn't curb it.

"I base it on the fact that this ranch requires all of my time and attention. There's no room in my life for anything else. I'm sorry if, in spite of my warnings, you convinced yourself that there was."

She wanted to belt him for the pity she saw in his eyes. Knock him off that saddle and onto the hard, bruising ground. She didn't have the strength. Instead, she lashed out with words that would hurt him more than physical pain. "Just like you've convinced yourself there isn't room in your life for your son?"

It was a cheap shot and it hit him like a hammer.

His eyes narrowed then glazed over with a torment that rivaled her pain. "My son is none of your business."

It was the final cut of the knife. "Just like your life is none of my business," she concluded in a small voice that begged him to come to his senses and deny it.

He didn't. "I had hoped that I'd made that clear."

"As crystal." Well, that was it. It was over. She looked down at her hands, clasped around the leather reins in a punishing grip, and knew she had to get out of there while she still had a scrap of pride left.

It took everything she had, but she brazened out a smile. "Well, cowboy, I guess this is it, then. It's been... interesting."

The silence was cut only by the creak of saddle leather and the constant sing of the wind as their gazes met and held for one final goodbye.

Her eyes blurred with tears, she reined Hester around, needing to get as far from him as she could get in the shortest amount of time.

He grabbed the reins and stopped her. Anger tempered with pain lanced through her. She forced herself to meet his wolf's eyes one last time. In that one last time, she read a war of emotions there—an anger that matched hers, a telling regret and even a shred of the love she knew he harbored but wouldn't let free.

"Dammit, Kelsey, I'm sorry. You knew how this would end, yet you kept coming back at me. You and your damned persistence." He looked away and swore. "I didn't ever want you here. I knew it would be a mistake. And it was. A big one.

"And let me remind you of something else," he continued as though, if he didn't say this now, he'd never get it said. "You came here for a story, not a romance. And with you, the story will always win in the end.

"Face it," he continued in a tone he tried to make soft but couldn't. "Playing Annie of the Wyoming sage would have bored you before long anyway. You wouldn't have lasted two months before you'd have remembered what brought you here, and you'd be on the first flight heading back to civilization, back to your daddy's newspaper and back to chasing your next hot lead."

She blinked back another threat of tears that blinded her to anything but the rancor in his words. "You've got this all wrapped up real neat and tidy, haven't you?" she lashed out, her outrage tempered with sadness. "You've had it mapped out from the beginning. How convenient. How utterly, perfectly convenient for you to form an opinion and stick with it no matter what.

"You know all about my kind, right? I'm the kind that will stop at nothing to satisfy my ambition. No matter that I forgot about my story the first time you kissed me. No matter that I'm the best thing to happen to you since sliced bread! What we shared was special."

"What we shared was great sex, Kelsey," he said, his voice hardening again with a resolve that his eyes backed up. "Nothing more."

She closed her eyes and clung to her heart's belief. "If, for one minute I believed that, I wouldn't be able to face myself in the mirror again. And if you believe it, then you're an even bigger fool than I thought," she added in a voice gone raspy with sorrow. Hearing it, she forced herself to toughen up.

"But you just go ahead and call it what you want, Caldwell. It's your story, tell it any way you want to."

She jerked the reins out of his hand. "Knock yourself out wallowing away here in your narrow-minded convictions. Keep telling yourself that something as powerful as what happens when we come together is nothing but sex. Keep convincing yourself what we could have together is something you want to factor out of your life.

"And since you're convinced it was just sex," she whispered with a vehemence that narrowed his eyes, "I hope you go to bed hard every night. I hope you go to sleep hurting and wake up every morning the same way. I hope you remember every touch, every kiss, every stroke of your body into mine and the love I felt for you when we came together."

Past reason, past pain, she shoved her hair out of her eyes. "And I sincerely hope you suffer because of it. Not just because I'm a poor loser. But because it doesn't have to be this way. It doesn't have to be me riding away. It doesn't have to be you sitting there watching me go."

But that's exactly how it was.

She rode away.

He watched her go.

At least she prayed he watched. And she prayed he was hurting even half as much as she was.

By the time she'd turned Hester over to Bax and his somber, searching eyes, all she wanted to do was throw her clothes in her suitcase and get out of sight of the Caldwell Cattle Company.

"Damn," she muttered as she jerked open the kitchen door and slammed it hard behind her. "Damn him and his—"

She stopped short when she spotted the startled expression of the woman watching her from the kitchen table.

"Oh. I'm sorry." Kelsey took a deep breath and made a concentrated effort to calm herself. That marginally accomplished, she returned the woman's curious stare and arrived at an unmistakable conclusion.

"Mrs. Caldwell?"

Donna Caldwell, a stylishly slim, regally attractive woman who, in her own way shared as many of Lucas's physical characteristics as the man who had fathered him, rose and extended her hand.

"Please, call me Donna. And you must be Ms. Gates. Kelly, wasn't it?"

"Kelsey," she corrected softly. "It's Kelsey."

"Of course," Donna Caldwell said, her tone apologetic. "Forgive me."

"No problem," Kelsey returned with a self-conscious attempt at a smile and a silent curse at a spiteful fate that had delivered her from one Caldwell to another.

"Forgive me for asking, dear, but are you all right?"

Kelsey ran a hand through her hair as the older woman took in the disheveled mess and her red face. Donna Caldwell was no doubt baffled by the way Kelsey had slammed into the kitchen like a crazed bull.

She was crazed all right. Crazed to have ever gotten in so deep.

"I'm fine. Really," she insisted, wanting nothing more than to get out of there. "And I'm sorry for barging in here like this. I . . . I was distracted."

"And madder than a hornet if I don't miss my guess."

Lucas's mother smiled kindly, and in that brief moment, Kelsey caught a glimpse of the smile Lucas was so hard-pressed to deliver and had such devastating effects when he did. "Has my son been giving you a hard time?"

She drew a breath of courage. "Actually, we, ah, we had just said our goodbyes," she hedged, clumsily sidestepping any dialogue that would lead to a discussion of Lucas. "I was about to pack and get out of everyone's hair."

"Oh, no. Oh, please," Donna insisted, taking Kelsey's hand and drawing her to the kitchen table. "I'm most anxious to talk with you. And Bax went to such great lengths to make sure you didn't leave until I returned."

"Bax? I don't understand," she said, easing reluctantly into a kitchen chair.

Donna fidgeted with a coffee cup, then filled one for herself, stopping short from pouring a cup for Kelsey. "Oh, I forgot. Bax tells me you drink tea. Could I brew some for you?"

Unsettled, but not quite connecting with why, she shook her head. "I'm fine, thanks. And I really do have to get going."

A soft rap on the door brought her head around.

Donna scrambled from the table, opened the door and let Bax inside.

"Ma'am," Bax said, as usual, his hat in his hands. Not usual was his smile. It was colored with an unease that set the hair on the back of Kelsey's neck on edge.

"Is there something going on here I should know about?" she asked, sensing a tension arch between Bax and Donna.

"Kelsey," Donna began, moving back to the table to confront her with a tentative hesitance, yet an underlying resolve. "My leaving just before you arrived wasn't an accident. I'd made a decision to disclose some information to you when you came for your interview. Information that will shock you and perhaps shock the entire nation when you divulge it in your newspaper."

Panic hit Kelsey like a bullet. Shock buffered its impact as she stared at Donna Caldwell, sensing she was about to tell her everything she had come here to find out. Something she no longer wanted to know.

In silence, she watched Donna glance at Bax, as if for support, before her soft golden eyes returned to Kelsey. "While I had made a decision, I'm afraid that at the last moment I got a bad case of cold feet."

"Mrs. Caldwell," Kelsey began, uncomfortable with the weight of the secrets that were about to be told. "I came here for a story on the leased land issue. I...I've gathered all the information I need to do the piece. While I appreciate your offer, it's not really necessary that I talk with you now."

Donna drew a deep breath and made herself look Kelsey in the eye. "I'm afraid it is necessary. And I'm afraid you don't have all the information. There's something else you need to know. Something, that if it comes to light, might be the one and only thing that will save the Caldwell ranching tradition, not to mention the ranching tradition as we know it in America today."

She glanced again at Bax. At his nod of encouragement, she continued. "I can't let something that my father and his father before him worked so hard to build be ruined. I can't let Lucas's hard work to maintain it be undermined. And I can't, in good conscience, protect my own selfish secrets any longer by keeping silent about a wrong that needs to be righted."

"Mrs. Caldwell," Kelsey began again as a rare and persistent urge demanded she stop this.

"No, dear. Don't stop me. It's taken me too long to get this far."

With that she rose, gathered the morning newspaper against her breast, then laid it out in front of Kelsey on the table.

Kelsey felt the blood drain from her face as she read the headlines.

Montgomery's A Winner, With His Family At His Side.

Her determination to avoid this conversation sank like a torpedoed ship as she studied the quarter-page photo of Harrison Montgomery. At his side, his wife, Helen, smiled with admiration, while Montgomery fondly embraced both Helen and their constant companion, his goddaughter, Dara Seabrook.

The Child He Never Had the caption read as the article went on to applaud Montgomery's devotion to his wife and goddaughter and, in turn, Dara's fervent support for the presidential candidate.

Slowly she lifted her head and met Donna Caldwell's eyes. The connection was vital and imploring. And she knew in that moment that Donna suspected Kelsey's true reason for searching out her son at the Triple C. She also knew that this article profiling the "perfect first family in the making" and the accompanying piece on Montgomery's stand for triple-digit increases of federal grazing land was the push that had shoved Donna Caldwell over the edge.

And while she couldn't fully experience the depth of Donna Caldwell's pain, she understood it. It was the pain a mother feels for her child. It was the pain she could no longer ignore.

Dara Seabrook wasn't Montgomery's child. Lucas was. Dara was only his goddaughter, the daughter of a deceased friend, with not even a hint of a blood tie. Yet it was Dara, the darling of the media with her glossy good looks and undying devotion, who was standing at his side. Standing at his side where Lucas rightfully belonged.

The injustice, which was both foul tasting and reeked of the cruelest twist of fate, didn't stop there. It wouldn't stop

unless someone stopped Montgomery. Because if someone didn't stop him, his proposed legislation could end up
threatening not only the Caldwell ranching legacy, it could
destroy his own son. It was the most bitter irony she could
possibly conceive.

With effort, Kelsey folded her hands together on the table and returned Donna's steady, determined gaze. With
regret, she, too, made a decision. "All right, Mrs. Caldwell," she said, knowing she was about to cross the final
line that would sever any chance of a future with Lucas.
"What is it you want me to know?"

Two hours later, both women were drained, both physically and emotionally. Kelsey had been peripherally aware
that Bax, his silent support no longer necessary, had
slipped quietly out of the house while she'd listened with
a bittersweet longing to Donna Caldwell's story.

It was a story of a young woman, a starry-eyed dreamer
who'd left the Wyoming family ranch to be the first Caldwell to earn a college degree. She was the same young
woman who had fallen in love with Harrison Montgomery's million-dollar smile and conquering hero pursuit.
Even as a twenty-year-old, Montgomery had been a man
whose undeniable charm could talk a naive young girl into
his arms and out of her virginity. It was a whirlwind
courtship that ended for him, at least, when the conquest
was over.

For Donna, it ended in the shame of an unplanned
pregnancy, and the pain of Montgomery's rejection when
he'd coldly offered to pay for an abortion even as he expressed his doubts to both his paternity and to whether she
was actually pregnant or just trying to trap him.

Barely nineteen, Donna had been devastated by his reaction, but too proud and independent to ask for help or

to insist on his acknowledgment. She'd dropped out of school and returned to the Caldwell ranch determined to raise her child alone. Alone except for a stern father who was ashamed of her and the bastard son whose parentage she refused to reveal.

The fear that Nathaniel Caldwell would make good on his threats to go after the father if he found out who he was, was one reason she kept her secret. Pride was another. She wanted nothing to do with a man who had so callously turned his back when she'd needed him. But her love for Lucas and a gradually escalating fear that Montgomery's wealthy and politically connected family might decide to take Lucas away from her if they found out about him, ultimately became her overriding concern.

The picture Donna painted grew bleaker and bleaker as Kelsey sat there, drawing her own conclusions that added insight to the loner Lucas had become. He'd been a child growing up, receiving conflicting messages from the adults in his life—reserved but steady love from his mother, grudging tolerance from his disappointed grandfather and a child's inherent awareness that his mother walked a fine line to keep the peace.

"When I first read about Harrison winning a senate seat," Donna was saying in a tone that bled pain through the resignation, "and then winning two more and finally, that he was seeking the presidency, I started tracking his political career a little more closely. Curiosity, I guess."

And the fact that you still loved him, Kelsey speculated as she watched Donna's face. She thought how ironic it was that they had shared the same kind of pain. The pain of knowing that the men they loved had rejected them.

"And maybe a little self-pity," Donna added with an honesty that dragged Kelsey back to the moment. "It was bad enough that he never acknowledged his obligation.

Maybe I'm to blame for not pushing harder. Lucas deserved better. I'll always feel guilty about that. Maybe if I'd forced the issue..." Her voice trailed off as her regrets resurfaced. Regrets that could not be assuaged at this late date.

"But I can do something now," she said with conviction. "I can do something for Lucas and for the industry. And you can help me."

Even though she'd known this was coming, Kelsey's gaze shot to hers.

"I need your help, Kelsey. I need you to print this story and expose Harrison for what he is. The voters need to know that he's a man who picks his obligations when they suit his purpose. A man who denied his own son and turned his back on a woman who needed him. If we can ensure his defeat with this disclosure, we may just ensure our own future."

Kelsey rose and walked to the window, looking toward the mountains for strength and guidance, as she'd often found herself doing.

"I don't know, Mrs. Caldwell," she said slowly as the full ramifications of the story hit her. "It was a long time ago. People idolize Montgomery now. He was a young man then. Youthful indiscretions are easier to forgive—especially when the wisdom of age has made up for past mistakes." She paused, listening to herself for the first time, sickened by what she was hearing.

Why was she trying to soft sell this all of a sudden when she was on the brink of a landmark story that would do everything for her career that she'd ever wanted? What had become of the go-for-the-jugular journalist who would have walked over hot coals for this kind of an exclusive?

Lucas Caldwell is what had happened. Lucas Caldwell had crossed her path and she'd never be the same again.

And this metamorphosis had been for what? If she could believe what he'd told her, he couldn't give a rat's rear end about her profession of love. If she could believe what he told her, all they'd shared was great sex.

This is the man she wanted to protect from public humiliation? This was the man she wanted to shelter from the cataclysmic deluge of press and TV coverage this story was sure to bring?

She turned slowly back to the woman who was watching her with a stark, determined intensity.

"Mrs. Caldwell," she began, meeting her eyes with a searching intensity of her own. "Does Lucas know about this?"

"Lucas knows."

The kitchen went deadly quiet as both women's gazes swung to the door. Kelsey's heart pounded out her shocked surprise as Lucas stepped into the room.

In a voice drained of emotion and as cold as winter, he repeated, "Lucas knows. And now that Ms. Gates knows, I imagine the whole world will know it, too."

Kelsey checked herself to keep from physically flinching when he pinned her with an accusatory look that proclaimed he'd been right about her all along.

"Congratulations, Kelsey," he said, his eyes and tone mocking the sentiment. "Looks like you finally got what you came for."

Ten

Her hat still hung on the rack...like her memory still hung in his mind.

She'd been gone ten days. Ten days and ten nights, Lucas reflected darkly as he swirled the last of the Amaretto in the bottom of the tumbler then downed it in one burning swallow.

He stared out the kitchen window at a sunset that should have moved him with its beauty. The streaks of red and hues of gold only made him think of her hair. In the honeyeyed warmth of the blended colors, he saw her smile.

He pushed away from the window and walked out of the kitchen. But there was no escape. Her scent still permeated his bathroom, the bedroom where they'd made love. Everywhere he turned, memories clawed at his gut like a currycomb, raking up feelings and wants and regrets that were better left dead and buried.

Not just feelings of them together. Older feelings. No less real, only further removed. Like his ten-year marriage to a woman as ill suited to the rigors of a rancher's life as Kelsey would be. Like the son he'd let Elise take away while he'd watched helplessly as she'd done it, hating himself every day since for letting it happen. Hating her money and the distance that kept him from his son—even, sometimes, hating the expectations that kept him anchored to the ranch.

And then there was the day, twenty years ago when he'd seen the grainy newspaper photo of Senator Harrison Montgomery in a Sheridan newspaper and he'd no longer had to speculate about who his father was.

He lay down on the bed in his darkening bedroom, folded his hands behind his head and remembered.

The resemblance had been shatteringly undeniable. He'd realized then that Montgomery was a mirror—if dated—image of himself, from his aggressively masculine looks to his broad-shouldered, raw-boned frame, to the dark, wavy hair and distinctively chiseled features.

Until that point, he'd always nurtured a brooding curiosity about his father, but his mother had been unapproachable on the subject. Confronting her with the photograph that day had been the easy part. His direction had been fueled by youthful outrage. Hearing her confirm his accusation, then dealing with Montgomery's disclaimer, had been hard and had ultimately molded him into the aloof loner he was today. And if he were being honest, it had also contributed to his hard-edged cynicism and the demise of his marriage.

A soft breeze drifted over his skin as he lay there. A cold resolve gradually reasserted itself as he admitted what he had to do. All the regrets in the world weren't going to change things. All the wishing that things could be different weren't going to make it so.

It was simple really. All he had to do was get on with his life. All he had to do was ride out the storm Kelsey's article was sure to stir up when she finally printed it and see past the pain of her betrayal.

After that, there was only one thing left: getting over her. He closed his eyes and drew a weary breath, wondering if he'd ever be able to dig deep enough to accomplish that one simple feat.

Kelsey loved her brother. It was a good thing because at the moment, it was the only thing that kept her from killing him.

"Grow up, Kelso. It's time, don't you think?"

"I didn't come here to be lectured. Especially not by you. You're nothing more than a misconnected child of the sixties. You're self-indulgent, self-possessed and spoiled beyond redemption. And you have the gall to tell *me* to grow up?"

She turned her back on her outrageously handsome sibling where he sat sprawled in all his brawny, sun-streaked glory in a canvas deck chair, her piece on Montgomery clasped loosely in his hand.

"You don't really want to print this," Jonas Gates the Third said, tossing the copy aside and rising.

She glared out over the deck of his beach house toward the ocean, unable to muster the anger to resist him when he wrapped his arms around her from behind.

"Kelsey, it's time you quit trying to prove yourself to the old man and go after what you really want."

"And I suppose you think I want that big jerk of a cowboy," she muttered, leaning back into his embrace, not knowing if she regretted or was glad she'd spilled out the whole sordid story about her feelings for Caldwell to this man who she loved with equal measures of devotion and exasperation.

He dropped a kiss on the top of her head. "Yeah. I think you want that big jerk of a cowboy. And I think the only thing keeping you from going to him is your pride. You can't snuggle up to pride on a cold winter night, Kelso. And you can't live your life in someone else's shadow."

"As if you have all the answers," she sputtered, loving him for caring, not wanting to get her hopes too high that he might be right.

She felt his grin against her hair. "Go to him, Kelsey. Give him another chance to experience the havoc you can wreak in his life."

"You're suggesting I go back to him, and you don't even know him."

"I know enough. Any man that can set you into this wild tailspin has to be a helluva man." He turned her in his arms to face him. "And, little sister, a woman like you deserves a helluva man."

He was a helluva man all right, Kelsey decided three days later as she waited for Caldwell in the bed they'd shared one glorious night that seemed like a lifetime ago.

Every minute that passed seemed like an additional millennium as second thoughts turned to thirds and she debated—for the thousandth time—the wisdom of her decision to come to him. Wisdom? If there had been an ounce of wisdom involved in her hurried trip back to the ranch, it was lost under pounds of irrational indiscretion, tons of hope and uncharted measures of love.

It had to be love. Nothing else could hurt this bad. Nothing else could have made her give up everything to come after Caldwell. And she had given up everything—

her job, her apartment, her breakthrough story, even her unhealthy but oddly familiar love/hate relationship with her father.

The day her father had called her into his office and demanded to know what she'd been up to, wasting her time and his money gallivanting to God knew where, was the day that had made the difference. Even more than her visit with her brother, that confrontation had been the turning point. As she'd stood there, listening to her father rail at her, she'd realized how convoluted their relationship had become. She'd held her story on Montgomery in her hand. All she would have to have done to silence him for once and for all about her inadequacies, would have been to hand it to him.

Yet, confronted with that undeniable victory, the importance of pleasing him had ceased to matter. What mattered was Caldwell, the man she loved. The realization had freed her. She'd laughed in her father's face and for the first time, it was a laugh laced with tolerant affection for the tyrannical dictator he'd always been.

"Dad," she'd said as she'd ripped the article to shreds and tossed it into his wastebasket, "go blow it out your ear."

Then, as he'd stood behind his desk in shock, she'd walked over to him, kissed him soundly on the cheek and put her arms around his stiffened frame. "I love you," she'd said, and experienced the joy of meaning it. "But I'm not putting up with your BS anymore." And then she'd left him with a grin and a wave and written out her resignation.

"One thing can be said about you, Gates," she said aloud, waiting for the panic to subside to a manageable level, "you not only burn your bridges, you blow them up behind you for good measure."

The final proof of that was the call she'd made to Beth Langdon that same day. She'd lied through her teeth to her friend. She'd told her she'd run into one snag after another and hadn't been able to prove their suspicions true. While Beth had been disappointed, relief over letting go of the last link to the story outweighed any guilt she felt. The ball was in Beth's court now. If Montgomery's campaign was going to go on the skids, Beth would have to find someone other than Lucas to be the catalyst.

In the meantime, Kelsey's only worry about the link between Lucas and Montgomery getting out was Willis Herkner. As Ed had predicted, the Weasel had been sniffing around.

A sound in the hall snapped her gaze to the door and back to the moment. A moment much more impactful than some obscure worry about what Herkner did or didn't know and what he would do with what he had.

Corny as it sounded, a greater moment of truth lay ahead. Her heart skipped as she remembered another night, another long, extended moment when she'd heard Caldwell's booted footsteps fall, then waited for him to come to her.

She didn't have to wait tonight.

The door flew open, slamming against the wall behind it with a force that knocked a print to the floor.

Her gaze swung from the fallen picture to the man standing like an angry bull in the doorway.

He looked positively combustible. And exhausted. And better than any man had a right to look, covered in trail dust, and with the dark shadow of a two-day beard, and enough raw, sexual energy to launch a guided missile.

She swallowed back her apprehension and pinned all of her hope on the fact that he also looked as miserable as she'd felt during the past two weeks.

"Rough day?" she ventured when he just stood there glaring at her as if he either wanted to throttle her or make hard, hot love to her.

"What the hell are you doing here?"

The words were a long time coming. And they were forced through vocal cords that sounded rusty from lack of use.

"It comes to me that we've played this scene before," she said, scooting to the side of the bed, demurely tugging her nightshirt with her as her toes touched the floor.

She saw in his eyes that he was remembering that other day, too, that other time he'd returned to the house and expected to find anything but her.

"You've heard of the bad penny?" she asked with a brave attempt at a smile. "We're related," she added, playing for his smile in return.

She didn't get one. If anything, his scowl deepened.

"That's what I like about you, Caldwell. You really know how to make a girl feel welcome. Give me a little help, would you? I'm dying here." What had started as one more bid to crack that iron mask of anger darkening his face, ended in a shaky plea, as every sensible bone in her body told her that coming back to him might have been the biggest mistake of her life.

"Caldwell?" Her voice faded to a small, defeated whisper as he turned his back on her.

He couldn't breathe. He couldn't think. Not past the wanting. Not past the need.

She'd done it to him again. With one look from those glittering green eyes, with one soft, vulnerable plea from those full, sensual lips, she had him courting ideas of love and everlasting and the sweet healing the warmth her body and spirit offered.

He wanted to hate her for her betrayal. He needed to hate her to save his sanity. Yet, as he stood there, stalled between the urge to run like hell in the opposite direction and to haul her beneath him on that bed, he only wanted to know why.

When he turned back to her, she met his gaze bravely, prepared to field whatever attack he launched. But he had no attacks left in him. He had only a need to know.

".Why, Kelsey? Why did you come back?"

She rose slowly, walked to the end of the bed and wrapped her hands around the bedpost, as if she needed it for support.

"Do you want the psychobabble bull or the straight scoop?" she asked hesitantly.

"By all means—give it to me straight."

She thought for a moment, then raised her face to his. "You know Lucy—Lucy in the *Peanuts* cartoon? You know how every fall she talks Charlie Brown into letting her hold the football for him? And how every year when he finally decides to trust her, she ends up doing her worst and pulling it out from under him?"

He sighed impatiently. "This is the straight scoop?"

"Straight as an arrow. What I'm trying to tell you is that for my whole life, I've been Lucy at her worst. I've been a bully, trying to prove my own self-worth by diminishing the worth of others. Always trying to get the attention and the acclaim my father never gave me."

She paused, gauging his silence as he leaned a shoulder against the door and heard her out.

"I've finally realized it's a little girl's game. A small person's goal. I don't want to be Lucy anymore. I want to be me. I want to please *me*. But the bottom line is—and this is the part you need to pay close attention to—I've discovered I can't be me without you—the man I want to please even above myself.''

Tears had gathered in her eyes as she watched him. A lump had expanded in his throat as he grappled with the desire to believe her and the need to keep his distance.

''I killed the story.''

His eyes narrowed.

''And I quit my job.''

He waited in an empty silence that became slowly crowded with a hope he had no right to entertain and an elation he had every reason not to feel.

''I also gave up my apartment. I love the mountains, Caldwell. I discovered when I went back to the city that I hated it there. In fact, I think I've always hated it. I just didn't know there was something else. Something better.

''I love the simplicity here,'' she hurried on, ''the honesty of the people. But most of all ... I love you.

''I love you,'' she repeated in a hushed but ardent whisper as she came to him, slipping against him like satin, sliding her hands around his neck with a tentative hopefulness that filled his chest with a love he no longer had the strength to deny.

''Are you going to run from me this time?'' she whispered as he sank into the love she offered. Wrapping his arms around her, he lifted her against him and turned his back on the denial that had held him captive.

''Go ahead,'' she murmured, trailing a string of licking, nuzzling kisses along his jaw as he laid her on the bed, then braced himself above her. ''Run. Run fast and run far. See how far it gets you.''

When her fingers fumbled, then stalled restlessly on his shirt buttons, he stood and handled the job for her.

Her eyes glistened with a thousand promises as he stripped the shirt from his shoulders, then eased down beside her on the bed.

"Do I take this to mean you're not running anymore?"

"I'm not running anymore," he whispered against the gentle rise of her breast. "I'm not running ever again, so you'd damn well better be sure about this."

Her moan told him how sure she was when he opened the buttons of her nightshirt and took her breast deeply into his mouth. He raised his head to see the flush of excitement on her cheeks, the beauty of her sweet, celebratory smile.

"I'm not running, Kelsey—but you'll understand if I still feel a little like Charlie Brown around you."

She smiled. "What you feel like," she murmured, helping him with his boots and britches, which they couldn't seem to get off fast enough, "is the man I want to spend the rest of my life making love to."

"Then why," he asked, unwrapping the single condom she'd placed on the stand by a single candle and rolling it on, "is there only one of these?"

She grinned, made room for him between her thighs, then gasped in pure, blissful pleasure when he slid deep inside her. "I didn't...ah...Caldwell...I didn't want you to think I was overconfident."

He worked on her confidence then. With the tantalizing stroke of his hands, the heated stroke of his body and a whispered pledge that promised, then delivered them both to a riot of sensual pleasure, then a peace sweeter than any either had ever known.

"Your mother is going to be disappointed."

The sun had long ago set, the loving had momentarily sated them, but the questions were not yet all answered.

He ran a long, callused but exceedingly gentle hand over the length of her back and drew her closer. "My mother has been trying to find a woman for me for years. When she finds out that woman is you, she'll be ecstatic. I wasn't the only one you made a lasting impression on during your brief visit."

Kelsey snuggled closer, loving the rich, earthy feel of a hardworking man and the lingering scent of their love-making that mingled beautifully with the exotic scents of ylang-ylang and sandalwood.

"I'm glad to hear she'll approve. But I was referring to her hope that I would run the story."

They both grew quiet then. Both reflecting on the reason she'd come to the Triple C in the first place. Both immersed in complex thoughts of repercussions, regrets and unknowns.

She raised up on an elbow and looked down at him. His eyes were soft and mellow, his dark curls lovingly mussed by her hungry hands only moments ago. In all, he was the most beautiful sight she'd ever seen. In all, she would die before she'd hurt or dishonor him. And in his eyes, she read his open acceptance of those undeniable truths.

"I think I've come up with another way to fight Montgomery on this leased land issue."

He looked at her with narrowed eyes.

"It's inevitable, you know," she said, touching a finger to his jaw then cupping his face in her palm. "You'll have to run for state representative."

She'd expected resistance. She was pleasantly surprised by his look of reluctant but resigned acceptance and knew he must have been giving it some thought.

"It doesn't appear to be something I can put off much longer," he said, confirming her suspicions.

"For the record, Caldwell," she said with a soft smile that relayed her approval, "I want to predict here and now that if Montgomery gets in as president, you'll beat him on the leased land increases. You'll make one heck of a great politician."

His eyes grew suddenly shadowed. "Yeah, well. As they say—'like father, like son.'"

There was no pride in the statement. Only a sad, poignant irony.

"It's his loss, Caldwell." She lowered her mouth to his and kissed him long and slow. "His greatest loss."

He turned her in his arms and tucked her head beneath his chin. "And you—you are my greatest find."

Tears stung her eyes, love swelled and nearly burst within her breast. "We're going to make a great team, you and I," she said when she could speak.

"What about your career?" he asked after a long moment, and she knew by the tension in his hands that it was a question lying heavily on his mind. "How can you walk away from it?"

"I'm not walking away from it. I figure you're going to need a good press secretary. Wouldn't you know it...?" She rose up on one elbow and grinned into his eyes. "I happen to know just the unemployed reporter with enough political savvy to fill that bill. I also figure the Sheridan newspaper can always use a free-lance correspondent."

When he looked away, his eyes still relaying a measure of doubt, she cupped his face in her hand. "Reporting is not my life, Caldwell. It's not even my avocation. It's something I enjoy but I can enjoy doing it anywhere.

"I've learned something through all of this. I don't have to please anyone but myself anymore. I don't feel the need. Someday, when we've got nothing better to talk about, I'll explain it to you. In the meantime, you're going to have to trust me on this. I'm exactly where I want to be. So let's go over this one more time for good measure.

"I'm nuts about you and you can ride to the end of the earth if you want to, but you are not going to be able to avoid me. So the question is, can you live with that knowledge? Can you live with me?"

"I guess I've crossed deeper rivers."

She elbowed him in the ribs.

"Okay. You want to hear it? Here it is. We are as different as night and day. All your life you've tried to live up to an image your father imposed, then made sure you didn't meet. All my life I've tried to ignore that fact that I was cast from the same stone as a man who turned his back on his obligations.

"Yet, through it all, what I really wanted was to grasp the sense that I belonged. To a family, to a tradition. My mother tried. In her own way, so did Elise. But no one, not even Bax, who is the closest thing to a father I've ever known, has ever made me feel inside the way you make me feel."

She swallowed hard. "And how do I make you feel?"

He touched a hand to her hair, then touched her heart through his eyes. "Whole. You make me feel whole. And I love you for it. Every wild red hair, every soft silken sigh. I love you, Kelsey, and I swear, if you hadn't come back here, I was coming after you."

The tears came then. Hot and salty as they slipped down her cheeks and against the chest of the man who gathered her against him.

This was love. This was joy. At its finest. At its fullest. And it made every chance she'd taken, every rule she'd broken, worth the effort and the pain.

He loved her again then. Slowly this time, with exquisite care and with astonishing attention to her physical needs. And when it was over and she could find the strength to speak, she offered her final gift.

"You need to know—I had one more act of bullying left in me before I left L.A."

Lucas rolled to his back, dragging her with him, positioning her gloriously languid weight until she was sprawled ever so provocatively across his body.

"Ah, well, I suppose old habits are hard to break."

He'd expected an answering grin from her. Instead, she raised her head, stacked her hands on his chest and propped her chin there.

"Kelsey? What is it?"

Her green eyes skittered to his and then away. "I, ah, I did some rather creative meddling before coming here, I'm afraid."

"Meddling?"

She nodded, pushed herself away from him and sat up cross-legged on the bed. She gathered the sheet to her breasts.

"Research has always been one of my strengths. Well, I did a little research on your ex-wife."

When he came up on an elbow she looked away. "Kelsey, what did you do?"

"I...I, ah, guess you could say I exercised the privileges my daddy's money can bring and, ah, finagled a little deal."

She snuck a peek at him from beneath her amber-tinged eyelashes, then plucked nervously at the sheet.

"A deal? Kelsey, will you just come out with it? You're beginning to make me nervous."

"Not half as nervous as I am."

He watched her, watched her draw a deep breath and set her mind to toughing this out.

"The long and the short of it is this—I found out that Elise's husband is senior partner in the law firm that handles all of my father's corporate legal business. Yeah," she agreed when his brows furrowed. "Small world.

"Anyway," she went on when he held a silence that invited her to continue, "I sort of dropped the heavy suggestion that if he didn't want to lose my father's legal business—and I'm here to tell you, it would be a major loss—that it might be wise if he convinced Elise that for everyone's best interest, she should let Cody see his father on a regular basis."

Her eyes were bright with both anxiety and dread, and for the life of him he could do nothing to relieve either. He was stunned.

He sat up, swinging his feet to the floor, and stared at the wall. After a deep breath, he raked his hands through his hair, still unable to speak, not daring to hope that what he'd believed was impossible might actually happen.

His son. He was going to see his son. To be a part of his life. To be the father he'd always wanted to be.

"Say something," she begged, in a voice so small and so full of an uncustomary tentativeness, he looked over his shoulder to her face.

"I...I don't know what to say."

"Say it's okay," she said, clambering across the bed on her knees and clasping her hands in his as a stunned smile finally broke out across his face. "Say that that little sorrel filly Bax is so sweet on would be a perfect match for a ten-year-old. Say you can't wait to see him because, Lucas, I made some mighty big promises before I left him yesterday."

"Left him? You saw him?"

"Oh, Lucas..." Her eyes misted over again with the sweetest shine, the softest glow. "It was like looking at you. It was like falling in love all over again."

With a whoop that startled a screaming giggle out of her, he wrapped her in his arms and tumbled her to her back on the bed. "You are a wonder."

"That's a fact," she agreed with a smile that matched his own, then laughed with a joy inherent to her nature until he silenced that laugh with a kiss.

"And you are my woman," he whispered against her mouth, loving her for her fire and her fury and her capacity to surprise him. "Kelsey... I don't know how to thank you."

Confident again in his love for her, she threaded her fingers through his hair. "I can think of a few ways. And I can think of a question I'd love to answer. But before you ask it, be warned—the answer is still yes."

"Yes?"

She nodded. "Yes."

"Well, in that case, Kelsey, would you... could you consider... moving your elbow? You're bruising the daylights out of my ribs."

Her eager anticipation changed in a heartbeat to a fiery and furious—though thoroughly staged—pout. "I was right about you all along, Caldwell. You are a jerk. And you pick the darnedest time to decide to display a sense of humor."

He laughed, realizing as he did, that a future with Kelsey promised to include a whole lot of laughing. "I'll work on my timing, okay? I promise. In the meantime—" he met her eyes, searched her face, amazed by the tenderness she inspired in him "—I love you, Kelsey. Marry me?"

Excitement darkened her eyes, then a hesitance made incredibly sweet by her lingering uncertainty. "You're finally sure that's the question you want to ask?"

He kissed her softly. "The only one."

"Then you already have my answer, Caldwell," she whispered, dragging his mouth back to hers. "The only one I've ever wanted to give you."

Enveloped in her love, enriched by her smile, he held her, heartbeat to heartbeat, man to woman, lover to friend. "And it's the only one I'll ever need."

*   *   *   *   *

Don't miss the exciting second book in the
SONS AND LOVERS *trilogy,*
REESE: THE UNTAMED, by Susan Connell,
coming next month from Silhouette Desire.

COMING NEXT MONTH

#979 MEGAN'S MARRIAGE—Annette Broadrick
Daughters of Texas
February's *Man of the Month* and Aqua Verde County's most
eligible bachelor, Travis Hanes, wanted Megan O'Brien as his
bride. And now that she needed his help, could Travis finally talk
stubborn Megan into being the wife he wanted?

#980 ASSIGNMENT: MARRIAGE—Jackie Merritt
Tuck Hannigan had to pose as pretty Nicole Currie's husband if
he was to protect her. Could this phony marriage get the
confirmed bachelor thinking about a honyemoon for real?

#981 REESE: THE UNTAMED—Susan Connell
Sons and Lovers
Notorious playboy Reese Marchand knew mysteriously sexy
Beth Langdon was trouble. But he couldn't stay away from the
long-legged beauty—even if it meant revealing his long-kept
secret.

#982 THIS IS MY CHILD—Lucy Gordon
Single dad Giles Haverill was the only man who could help
Melanie Haynes find the baby she'd been forced to give up
years ago. Unfortunately, he was also the one man she could
never love....

#983 DADDY'S CHOICE—Doreen Owens Malek
Taylor Kirkland's goal in life was to regain custody of his
daughter. But then he met Carol Lansing—an irresistible woman
whose love could cost him that dream....

#984 HUSBAND MATERIAL—Rita Rainville
Matthew Flint never thought he would make a good husband—
until he lost the only woman he ever loved. Now he would do
anything to convince Libby Cassidy he really was husband
material.

Take 4 bestselling love stories FREE

Plus get a FREE surprise gift!

Bestselling author

RACHEL LEE

takes her Conard County series to new heights with

A CONARD COUNTY Reckoning

This March, Rachel Lee brings readers a brand-new, longer-length, out-of-series title featuring the characters from her successful Conard County miniseries.

Janet Tate and Abel Pierce have both been betrayed and carry deep, bitter memories. Brought together by great passion, they must learn to trust again.

"Conard County is a wonderful place to visit! Rachel Lee has crafted warm, enchanting stories. These are wonderful books to curl up with and read. I highly recommend them."
—*New York Times* bestselling author
Heather Graham Pozzessere

Available in March, wherever Silhouette books are sold.

FRIENDS, LOVERS...AND BABIES
by Joan Elliott Pickart

The Baby Bet

Joan Elliott Pickart brings her own special brand of humor to these heartwarming tales of the MacAllister men. For these three carefree bachelors, predicting the particulars of the MacAllister babies is much easier than predicting when wedding bells will sound!

In February 1996, the most romantic month of the year. Ryan MacAllister discovers true love—and fatherhood—in *Friends, Lovers...and Babies*, book two of THE BABY BET.

And in April 1996, Silhouette Special Edition brings you the final story of love and surprise from the MacAllister clan.

BABBET2

Trained to protect, ready to lay their lives on the line, but unprepared for the power of love.

Award-winning author Beverly Barton brings you Ashe McLaughlin, Sam Dundee and J. T. Blackwood... three rugged, sexy ex-government agents—each with a special woman to protect.

Embittered former DEA Agent Sam Dundee has a chance at romance in GUARDING JEANNIE, IM #688, coming in January 1996. Hired to protect Jeannie Alverson, the woman who saved his life years ago, Sam is faced with his greatest challenge ever...guarding his heart and soul from her loving, healing hands.

And coming in April 1996, the trilogy's exciting conclusion. Look for J. T. Blackwood's story, BLACKWOOD'S WOMAN, IM #707.

You're About to Become a

Privileged Woman

Reap the rewards of fabulous free gifts and benefits with proofs-of-purchase from Silhouette and Harlequin books

Pages & Privileges™

It's our way of thanking you for buying our books at your favorite retail stores.

PROOF OF PURCHASE
SD-PP91
Offer expires October 31, 1996

Harlequin and Silhouette—
the most privileged readers in the world!

For more information about Harlequin and Silhouette's PAGES & PRIVILEGES program call the Pages & Privileges Benefits Desk: 1-503-794-2499

Silhouette®

SD-PP91